I072565b

ANGUISH UNFOLDS

BOOK 2 OF THE NATURE'S FURY SERIES

*Sometimes the storms in your mind
rage stronger than anything in nature.*

A.E. FAULKNER

4700 Millenia Blvd.
Ste #175-90776
Orlando, FL 32839

info@indieowlpress.com
www.indieowlpress.com

ANGUISH UNFOLDS

Cover design by Michelle Preast
Indie Book Cover Designs / Michelle-Preast.com

Interior layout by Vanessa Anderson
at NightOwlFreelance.com

Manufactured in the United States of America

Paperback ISBN-13: 978-1-949193-63-3

This book is dedicated to all those who forge the path they were ultimately meant to follow, no matter what challenges attempt to slow or stop them.

"It's the end of the world every day, for someone."

— *Margaret Atwood, The Blind Assassin*

Contents

Contents

ANGUISH UNFOLDS

Chapter 1

The firelight dances across my vision as my head melds into a folded gray sweatshirt. Tonight's pillow. Aidan and Jeff had warned us it would be cold sleeping outside at the campground serving as their temporary home, but now that I'm snuggled up in a red fleece blanket, I really don't care. While adrenaline initially fueled this evening's adventure, my brain and body are calling it a day.

My heavy eyelids flutter closed, snuffing out my view of the mesmerizing flames. I'm transported to the place my dreams always take me—home. My mind traipses through memories of holidays, birthday parties, and vacations. However, the respite from reality disappears in what seems like seconds.

Yanking me from my memories, a vice-like grip jerks my shoulders upright, tossing my head back in a whiplash motion. A rough hand closes over my mouth while a strong arm wraps around my body, directing my focus upward.

The dying flames throw just enough light onto the grimacing face to render it recognizable. Jim stands over my sleeping sister, one hand pressed to his mouth, pointer finger over his lips in a silent, "Shhhh." His other hand is directed toward Quinn, a reflective glint flashes off the knife he grasps.

My groggy brain is slow to process what's happening. A cool night breeze washes over me, alerting my senses to the immediate danger. A single tear slips down my cheek as realization overwhelms me. They can do whatever they want to hurt us right now and there's nothing I can do about it.

Hot breath meets my ears as Dan whispers, "Stay quiet, Riley. We just wanna talk to you. Let's get up slowly."

I nod slightly in acknowledgement.

Dan's grip loosens, but Jim's cold eyes lock on me as I slowly rise. Trembling, my mind tingles with questions. What do they want with me? Why does Jim have a knife? Would they listen if I tried to talk them out of whatever it is they're doing? What would happen if I scream right now? Would Aidan, Jeff, and Wes run out here and stop Jim and Dan from whatever they're doing?

I slowly turn toward Dan, who now stands behind me. His scowl confirms that Jim's anger is contagious. In the waning firelight, Dan motions toward Jim and nudges my shoulder forward. I turn in time to see Jim creep away from our sleeping area, one sure-footed step at a time. I quietly follow, turning back to glance at Quinn's sleeping form before we reach the path leading out of the campground.

Jim's steps transform into stomps the farther we get from Quinn and the ramshackle cabins. By the time we reach the campground's entrance, Jim's fury erupts. Turning on his heel, he charges toward me.

Startled, I back up and crash into Dan. Cowering from both guys, a choked yelp escapes my throat.

Alarm and pity sweeps across Dan's features.

"Riley! What are you doing here? And why the hell did you steal our bikes?" Jim barks, a blast of breath floating toward my nose.

Beer. He's been drinking tonight. I never thought he was as bad as Quinn always said, but I'm not liking this drunk version of him. Dropping my gaze to the ground, I wrap my arms around myself. "I… I…"

"Calm down. You're scaring her," Dan interrupts. His effort is short-lived when Jim throws a finger in his face, pointing. "You stay out of this. I'm handling it." Without hesitation, Dan backs away, his eyes landing on the overgrown dirt path.

"Riley!" Jim wraps his meaty hands around my shoulders, the movement drawing my eyes to meet his. Anger and accusation reside in his deep brown irises. Lies flash through my mind. I can't tell Jim the truth. He's already furious, and maybe a little drunk. The last thing I want is to push him further.

"Jim, we um, we just came here to get away for a few hours," my quaking voice calms slightly as the lies roll off my lips. "We… we borrowed your bikes, but we thought we could get them back to you before you even noticed."

Pointing back toward the cabins he demands, "Who are those guys?"

"Th-they're just people Quinn met," I stammer. My voice is hesitant as my mind races. "Wait, how did you know we were even here? And with other people?" My eyes narrow in question while Jim's widen in momentary alarm.

"Don't you worry about that right now," Jim snipes, recovering quickly. "Dan, get the bikes. We're going home. We can all talk back there."

I shake my head in protest. "I can't just leave Quinn. Look, I'll answer whatever you want. Let's talk here and then you can just take your bikes home. Quinn and I will find a way back." My eyes volley back and forth between the guys. Dan remains fixated on the ground.

Jim crosses his arms. "Sorry, Ri, that's not going to work. You're coming with us."

What? With rekindled adrenaline fueling my tired muscles, I turn on my heel and run, pushing my legs to launch me as far away as possible. Just as the first cabin comes into view, a shoulder collides with my back in a tackle. My knees and palms break the fall, skidding in the dirt. Tiny rocks tear into my skin, lodging themselves within. A firm grip yanks me around, bringing me face-to-face with Jim.

"Not happenin', Ri," he says, his voice low and steady. He jabs a thumb toward the cabins and the dwindling campfire. "You don't cooperate, someone's gonna pay and first in line is your sister." His dark eyes narrow as he leans in closer. Warm breath, reeking of beer, stings my nose. "You have no idea what I'm capable of."

Oh, but I think I do. And I just got confirmation of it.

Chapter 2

I solemnly follow Dan and Jim as they walk the bikes out to the main road. Jim made it clear that I am to remain quiet and compliant. If I run, they'll just catch me. If I scream, they will hurt anyone who gets in their way.

When we reach the road, Dan throws a leg over one bike while Jim motions for me to climb on the back of his. Defeated, I gingerly slink onto the seat and wrap my arms around Jim. He starts the bike and tears off down the road.

As the wind blasts my face, I struggle to hold back tears. We're just going back to Jim and Dan's trailer to talk for a little while. Then they'll bring me back here to Quinn. I replay these thoughts in my mind until I almost believe them.

Jim and Dan deftly swerve around the trucks, cars, and SUVs frozen in a gridlocked graveyard. They must have done this a hundred times since the crash. Dropping my head forward,

I squint my eyes shut and block out the death and destruction surrounding me.

Debris rests on the road at scattered intervals, as if forever abandoned by its former owners: a stuffed teddy bear, a flattened baseball cap, the crunched remains of sunglasses. A hint of oil and gasoline wafts in the air, but mostly the air is tainted by an underlying rot. I don't want to think about what's causing that smell.

When the bike slows to a walking pace, I peek at my surroundings. Just outside the trailer park, some of the wreckage has been cleared away. How did I not notice this when Quinn and I were riding out of here with Aidan and Jeff? Maybe I was too focused on exhilaration fueled by freedom and a plan. That might explain why dread is enhancing my situational awareness.

As we cruise through the trailer park at a snail's pace, I notice dim lights in some of the windows. So there are others here. I guess they're keeping to themselves like Quinn and I did. I release a heavy sigh as thoughts of my sleeping sister flutter through my mind. I pray she doesn't notice that I'm gone. It would send her into a terrible panic. I can still make it back before she wakes up. I'll just get this over with and maybe Dan can take me back to the campground.

When the guys park their bikes, the engines stutter to silence and we all climb off. I follow Jim, close on his heels, to the front door. Dan trails uncomfortably behind. With a sense of purpose, I stride through the front door as Jim's shadow.

"Well, I'm glad to see you perked up, Ri," Jim commends.

Dan slowly wanders into the trailer and closes the door.

Crossing my arms and plopping down on the couch, I decide

to be honest. A little bit anyway. "Look, guys, let's have our talk and then I really need to get back to Quinn. I mean, if she wakes up and I'm not there, she's going to freak out."

Jim and Dan share a sideways glance before joining me on the worn gray couch.

"How did you even find us?" I ask, wrapping my arms around myself. Dan barely looks at me. He knows this is wrong, but his loyalty to Jim must be stronger than his conscience.

"Well, you see, Riley," Jim starts sharply. "We don't take kindly to strangers sneaking around the trailer park. And that's exactly what those rats you were with did."

"What?" I ask shakily. "What are you talking about?"

Jim stops short and turns toward me. "Riley, what were you doing with those guys? How do you even know them?"

"I don't really know them…" I stammer. "Quinn met Aidan a few days ago. He and his friends were kind of in the same situation as us. Stranded. Trying to get home." I stop, not wanting to say too much and give him information that he'll use against us.

"Well, we saw them nosing around the trailer park," Jim explains. "So we followed them home one night." He nods toward Dan, smirking. "Wanted to see where the rats were nesting." With this little bit of reassurance, Dan moves to stand next to his brother.

My eyes widen. Wait, Jim and Dan were watching Aidan and Jeff? Do they know that the guys came to Aunt Grace's trailer to talk to us?

"So," Jim continues. "We figured we'd teach them a lesson about sneaking around and stealing people's stuff." I focus on holding my features expressionless while my brain screams that Jim and Dan were doing the exact same thing at the trailer park. Not that I'm going to call them on it.

"Yeah," Dan chuckles. "We were just about to show them that we own that trailer park!" Jim elbows Dan in the ribs, promptly shutting him up.

With no hesitation, Jim explains. "We planned to pay the rats a little visit, but wouldn't you know, Riley, our bikes were gone. Along with you and Quinn." Narrowing his eyes, he taps his chin as if contemplating this information for the first time. "I'd say that's a mighty big coincidence."

Inhaling a deep breath that fails to slow my rapid heartbeat, I push words out of my mouth. "I told you, Jim. We…we just wanted to borrow your bikes for the night and get away." Yeah, that's believable. When did I become so good at lying? It spurs me to continue. "You know we were cooped up in Aunt Grace's trailer for so long. We had to just get out and see what the world outside our door looked like."

He raises an eyebrow, assessing my lie. A minute later, satisfied with my response, he passes a slight nod to Dan. While Dan holds his gaze, no words pass between them. Turning back toward me, Jim's agitation has dissolved, and his expression softens.

"Riley, we gotta get outta here," he implores. "Things aren't great now but they're gonna get worse. This weather, it's changing. And the problems it's causing, well, the authorities can't keep up with it."

Dan chimes in, lending his support to Jim's theory. "Yeah, Riley. Route One still isn't cleared all the way. If we stay here, the people that can't get out for supplies, well they're gonna start takin' them, if you know what I mean. And you don't want to be around for that."

Tag-teaming, Jim announces his solution. "But you don't have to worry, Riley, 'cause we have a plan." Looking at each other momentarily, both guys break into a grin and slide their eyes my way. "And we want you to be a part of it," Jim says, smirking.

Chapter 3

The guys brim with pride as confusion and fear sweep through me. Before words form, I slowly shake my head back and forth. Shifting my eyes between Jim and Dan, I push past the sinking feeling in my gut and find my voice. "Guys, I...I need to get back to Quinn now."

Crossing his arms, Jim's expression sours in disappointment. "Now, you haven't even heard us out yet. At least listen to our idea."

"And you know, I tried to talk to you about this before. Before you just took off with our bikes," he says, pointing between him and Dan. "Did you even get my note? I told you we needed to talk."

Burying my face in my palms for a moment, I contemplate my answer. I really don't care about any of this right now. I just wanna get back to that campground before Quinn wakes up.

"Yes, I got it. I just…didn't get a chance to…everything happened so fast and…I just. I don't know."

Pushing back into the worn cushions, I smooth my goose-bumped arms. My eyes refuse to meet Jim's or Dan's. They flit around the room as if the walls will inch closer if I look away. Movement catches my eye outside the living room window and the hair on the back of my neck prickles as if I'm being watched. When I squint at the window to better my focus, the voices around me mute.

I'm startled out of my seat when a hand flicks in front of my face, fingers snapping loudly. "Riley! Pay attention, we're trying to talk to you," Jim commands.

"Sorry, go on." I'm sure it was nothing. Just let them talk and then figure out a way to get back to the campground.

Jim heaves out a frustrated breath and glares at me. Rubbing his stubbly chin, he cuts to the point. "Riley, here's the plan." Just as quickly as his anger flared, his features soften. He drops a knee to the floor in front of me as if proposing. "Dan and I are headin' south. To Langley Air Force Base. We're gonna stay there until everything here is cleaned up."

Narrowing my eyes in confusion, I question, "That's a good plan. I'm glad you guys figured out what to do. But why'd you have to bring me here to tell me that?"

Meeting my eyes intently, he declares, "Cuz, Riley, you're coming with us."

My protests fall on deaf ears. Jumping to my feet, I plead my case. "I can't go!" My eyes bounce between Dan and Jim with each word. "I need to get back to my sister. I need to be with her." My hands fly together, wringing uncontrollably.

I see the moment Dan's conscience cracks. His nervous eyes shift to his brother. Scratching his head in an attempt to appear casual, he murmurs. "Maybe we should just take her back to that campground and get on our way."

Hope surges through me. Briefly.

Jim's emotionless eyes remain fixed on me as he mutters, "Shut the hell up, Dan." Although I've never been close enough to confirm this, I've heard that a shark's eyes are soulless. As if they harbor deep nothingness. That's what I see in Jim's dark irises.

Hot tears spring to my eyes when he steps toward me, grasping my shoulder and leaning closer. "Now you listen to me, Riley. Quinn is not a part of this. I am not putting up with her shit ever again. She can go back home, and she'll be just fine."

Sorrow slides down my cheeks as he releases his grip and swipes a somber mask over his features. How does he transform from raging to sympathetic in a heartbeat? Could he be mentally ill?

Glancing at Dan, he sighs and runs a hand through his short dark hair. He turns back toward me with a much softer expression.

"Hey, it'll be okay. We'll figure this out." A sappy smile washes over Jim's face and his voice lowers to a whisper. "You know, Riley, I always thought we were meant to be together. Even when we were little kids."

With those words, my stomach twists in fear and uncertainty.

Jim insists that we all get some rest before we start this journey. He doesn't want to drive overnight. While Dan retreats to his bedroom, Jim throws a blanket on the couch for me.

"We'll sleep out here," he says, eyeing me. "Just so you don't get any ideas. I know what you're thinking." He releases a sigh. "If you can just get back to the campground, you and Quinn can hightail it outta here, right?"

I remain silent, unmoving. It's the only thing I'm in control of right now.

"Well, we'd just go right back there. This time on our bikes, so we'd get there much faster. And I really don't think you'd want to see what could happen."

My teeth tremble but I purse my lips closed to silence them. There's no way I can form a syllable without crumbling into a blustering mess of tears. How is this happening? This isn't the Jim I grew up with. This is the person that Quinn has always seen.

I burrow under the flannel blanket and meld into the couch. I just want to disappear.

My mind runs through scenarios that would take me back to the campground. At some point, it must have slowed to a useless churning because the next thing I know, a deep voice rouses me from a dreamless sleep. "Riley. Wake up!" Dan greets me, his eyes cautious. "It's time to go. Jim wants to get on the road with the first light."

I pull myself up and begrudgingly get ready. I don't ask what time it is. I don't care. Dawn breaks and the sun slowly spreads its fiery rays over the land. The guys gobble down some strawberry Pop-Tarts. I just break mine into smaller pieces, so it looks like I'm eating. I swallow a bite or two but the lack of hunger I faced when Quinn and I first got to the trailer park returns.

Loaded up with as much as we can carry on our backs, we

return to the bikes. The guys must have been planning for this. I don't even know if there's anything for me in those bags. They were sitting by the door, just awaiting this road trip. And my bag, which carries all that I own at this moment in time, sits back at the campground with my unsuspecting sister.

The back of my neck tingles as a shiver sprints up my spine. It stems from something other than the dread pitting in my stomach. I feel eyes on us. Turning my head from side-to-side, I search for the source. Maybe someone sees us and will help me.

"Let's go!" Jim barks. With one last look, my eyes land on a nearby bush. Its full leaves tremble but it's probably just the wind. No one's coming to rescue me.

Without a word, I throw a leg over the back of Jim's bike. Is this really happening? A moment later, the bikes rev to life and shoot toward the highway. The standstill of cars and trucks is merely a blur.

My anxiety skyrockets with each mile carrying me farther away from my sister. And farther away from home. My home will never be with Jim and his brother. If I can just get away, I can go back to the campground and get Quinn. We'll walk the whole way home if we have to.

I pinch my eyes shut to hold back the tears threatening to spill. The truth stings. I have zero ability to get myself out of this situation.

Chapter 4

We drive south on Route One. The sea air invades my nose, reminding me of why my family came here in the first place. I glance toward the ocean, catching flashes of the salty waves between hotels and restaurants lining the highway.

My eyes catch the Grotto Pizza sign as we speed past it. We always ate there—several times during each vacation because we all loved that spiral-sauced pie so much. When we pass The Carousel hotel, I squint my eyes closed to trap any tears that are plotting to spill.

The enormous building, practically touching the clouds, actually houses an ice rink. An ice rink at the beach. Every summer Quinn and I would beg our parents to take us there. And they did, until we got too old for it—or maybe just too big. The hotel ceased reaching the clouds and the patch of ice seemed to shrink, barely big enough to accommodate us and any others with figure skating dreams.

Dan trails just a few feet behind us. His reflection zooms along the fancier buildings with mirrored exteriors. Fighting to push regret-filled thoughts from my head, I focus on watching him.

As we pass the city limits and near Interstate 95, the concrete, steel, and glass give way to trees, bushes, and grass. I glance over my shoulder every few minutes, keeping an eye on the focal point Dan and his bike have become. I can't do this alone, and Dan's the only one who can help me now. Or at least maybe keep Jim calm.

The interstate has much prettier scenery, but it's not as interesting as the city. When we reach a long stretch of nothingness, I turn to see Dan's bike falling back. Either we're going faster or he's slowing down. Taking another peek behind us, his bike slows until it sputters to a stop.

Jim's voice pulls me from the scene behind us. "Riley! Stop moving around so much. You're throwing the damn bike off balance!"

Gripping Jim's shirt, I screech in his ear. "Dan's stopping. We have to turn around!" Stealing a glance over our shoulders, Jim huffs out a few obscenities. The sudden deceleration slams my body into his back. We turn and speed back to Dan.

Rolling to a stop, Jim shuts the bike off and stomps over to where Dan stands with his motionless bike. Attempting to recapture the air flushed from my lungs, I stumble after the guys, arriving in time to hear Jim reprimanding his brother.

"What the hell happened?" Jim asks, inspecting the bike. He huffs out a deep breath and shakes his head.

"I sorta ran out of gas," Dan says meekly, raising a fist to his mouth as if stemming any further explanation. Anticipation smothers the air. Sweat beads on my neck, preparing to race down my back. I expect Jim to erupt. Rage radiates from his narrowed eyes, but his voice is low and calm. Somehow it feels more threatening than if he was shouting.

"I got the bags ready. Your job was to prep the bikes—"

"I know, I know, I screwed up, okay?" Dan counters. "Damn gauge is busted. It's not readin' right."

After a few awkward minutes of silence, Jim announces our new plan.

"Since you couldn't get the job done, I'll do it," he says, glaring at Dan. "You two stay here. I'll ride to the nearest gas station and siphon some gas. Then maybe we can get back on the road."

My pulse eases as understanding dawns that I don't have to go with him. Or that Dan is going, leaving me alone with Jim.

"How you gonna do that?" Dan asks. "You don't even have—"

"Don't you worry about it. If it wasn't for your sorry ass, I wouldn't have to, but I'll figure it out." Jim staggers toward his bike, throwing one last glance over his shoulder at us. "Just stay put. I'll be back soon. Stay out of sight."

Hope blossoms in my chest. Is fate intervening, trying to help me get back to my sister?

With that, he throws a leg over his bike and revs the engine, kicking up dust when the tires spin. Dan and I stand next to each other and watch him disappear into the distance.

"Should we maybe move the bike to the side of the road and try to find some shade?" I ask Dan innocently. This is my chance.

Maybe I can convince him to just let me go. I never thought Jim would leave my side so soon.

"Yeah, I guess we should. You know, I didn't plan on making this whole trip." He waves a hand around in the air as if being here is an inconvenience.

"Well, you know, Dan," I start cautiously. "I didn't plan on it either. And I wasn't really given a choice, you know?"

He narrows his eyes at me as if I'm transparent. Okay, maybe he isn't as dumb as Quinn always said he was. I start to plead my case when he raises his pointer finger in the air to shush me.

"Do you hear that?" he asks intently. All I hear is the strained silence between us.

"I don't hear anything," I say. "So, Dan, I was saying—"

"Riley, shush," he says, turning to look down the road before us. He raises a hand in the air, silently telling me to stay quiet. This time I do hear something.

A low rumbling resonates in the distance. What is that? Instinctively, I clasp my hands together, wringing them.

Dan catches the movement and smirks. "You know Jim says you look like a damn lunatic when you shuffle your hands like that."

I drop them to my thighs and shoot Dan a sneer.

He meets my gaze but his eyes flash with worry. "Whatever it is, it's getting louder. Something's coming."

Chapter 5

Cupping my hands around my forehead, I form a shade barrier in a useless attempt to get a better view. Dan startles me when he swats my arm.

"Hey, let's blend in with the green. It's better if we see who's coming before they see us."

I nod in agreement.

We survey our surroundings, mentally inventorying our options. Trees line the highway, but they are set back from the road. I can't tell how much time we have before they get here, whoever they are.

I didn't notice when we stopped passing restaurants, gift shops, mini golf places and hotels, but there are no buildings to hide within or behind at the moment.

"How about that bush?" I ask, pointing at an overgrown hydrangea a dozen feet from the road.

Dan nods, then takes off for his downed bike. I spring into action. I want to be hidden before whatever is coming gets here.

Positioning myself behind the flourishing shrub, I watch Dan clumsily roll the bike a few feet behind me. Other than a few shooting rays reflecting from the bikes' metal, the tall grass mostly conceals it.

This whole area is stunning. I hadn't noticed it before, but the rich brown tree trunks climb to the sky, their sturdy arms smothered in emerald leaves. Smaller white-flowered trees hang in the background as if hiding behind their older siblings.

I kneel beside Dan. The rumbling grows louder, like a massive swarm of bees descending upon us.

"I don't see nothin' yet. Do you?" Dan asks.

Turning toward him, I shake my head. Maybe I need a better angle.

Just as the rumbling crescendos to a mechanical roar, I peek around the side of the bush, gently brushing aside the curtain of fragrant blooms. Like an oasis flickering in the shimmering waves of heat, a boxy vehicle rises on the horizon. Mirror images trail it, each growing bigger as they get closer.

A convoy.

"It's the military," I whisper, though I'm not sure why. Dan probably can't hear me over the approaching grumble. And there's no way anyone in those vehicles would hear us talking.

"Let's flag them down. Maybe they can help us!" My voice rises with my excitement. This could be my chance to escape.

"Now just hold up!" Dan says impatiently. "Jim told us to wait here." He pauses, probably trying to imagine Jim's voice in his head, directing him on what to do.

I don't need his permission. Heck, no one asked my permission to bring me here. Rising to my feet, I decide to make a run for it. At least Jim isn't here to tackle me to the ground again. As I draw in a deep breath to ready my lungs, a soft hand lands on my arm.

"Stay hidden," his voice softens. "Let's just watch and try to figure out who they are."

I cross my arms and sulk. I can already tell who they are. Who else drives in formation in a line of boxy green Humvees? Still, I stay hidden and watch, thrusting an arm into the bush, separating branches just enough to give me a line of sight.

As the trucks roll closer, I will my eyes to capture every useful detail. Each truck is a mirror image of the one before it. Camouflaged soldiers fill each vehicle, an occasional green-clad arm resting on an open window as they filter past us.

They all look pretty standard to me. The only thing to catch my eye is the large block letters on the back of each Humvee. The black, no-nonsense font reads: United States Armed Forces. Then under that, in smaller letters: Department of Operational Assets: Resources, Infrastructure & Population.

Geez, could that name be any longer? I wonder if they're headed to the Air Force base, too? I mean, their job is to serve and protect. Or is that the police? Either way, I bet they're on the way to help people. And maybe they'd help us too. Or me. Dan and Jim already have a plan and they don't need me for it.

I glance at Dan, who's watching the convoy intently. "Come on, let's flag them down before they're gone!" I say, louder this time. Pushing back from the branches, I stand tall, looking at him expectantly.

Anger flashes in his eyes like lightning. "Now I told you, Jim said to stay put. We go out there now and he'll kick both of our asses." As if sensing my disbelief, he wraps a strong hand around my elbow. "I mean it, Riley. Stay put. Who knows where the hell they'd take us?"

My slow nod promises I won't run. I didn't think of that. They're heading in the direction we were going, but that's the opposite of where I want to go. What if I flagged them down and they just loaded me up on a vehicle and continued on their mission? I'd still be moving farther away from home.

Convinced I'm a willing hostage for the moment, Dan releases my arm. We both meld into the bushes and watch as the convoy continues down the road, kicking up dust and scattering stones in its wake. By the time the last of the convoy snakes out of sight, a chill pulses through me.

I thought this was a chance to escape, but icy fingers claw at the back of my neck in warning. Goosebumps bloom along my forearms. A moment ago, I was daydreaming about the sweltering sun, and now I'm practically shivering. Something about this doesn't feel right.

Chapter 6

Dan's forehead beads with sweat, but that doesn't mean much. The heat is stifling, and he's not exactly dressed for warm weather. He and Jim both wore jeans and black t-shirts for this trip. Now that I think of it, I actually haven't seen either of them wear shorts in years. I can't imagine how warm Dan must be.

Although I'm thankful that I wore tan shorts and a lilac t-shirt—colors that should reflect the light—the sun's cruel rays scorch my fair skin. When we'd play at the beach as kids, Quinn's skin was always sun-kissed by the end of the day. Mine was singed to an angry red if I ventured out from the shade of our blue-and-white-striped umbrella for more than five minutes.

Silence settles around us, along with the dust and stones on the road. It must be early afternoon by now. We haven't made it very far, but that's fine with me. We're definitely still in Maryland.

It wasn't that long ago we passed the hotels and restaurants lining Ocean City.

Tired of my own thoughts, I decide to strike up a conversation with Dan. Now that we're alone, maybe I can broach some topics I'm sure Jim would never allow.

"Dan, can I ask you something?" I cautiously proceed. His guard must be at least a little weakened without Jim here commanding him, and I may be taking advantage of that, but I'm willing to accept any resulting guilt. Swiping his sweaty forehead, he nods in affirmation.

"That night Quinn and I had dinner at your place…"

His eyes widen for a moment before fixating on me. "What about it?"

As if on cue, my hands clasp together and start their wringing dance.

"What did you serve as the meal?" I attempt to cough out my nervousness. "I mean, what was that meat?"

He gives me a sideways glance and wipes his damp hair off his face.

"What does that matter? That was before—who cares?"

"I care," I start with a shaky voice. "Because I've basically been kidnapped by two people who I thought I knew." I pause for a moment, taking a deep breath. "I need to know what they are truly capable of, because I never thought they were capable of this." Tears threaten to punctuate my statement. I do not want to cry in front of Dan, or Jim, for that matter. I bite my lip, attempting to use physical pain as a distraction.

Dan huffs out a deep breath and rubs his temples as if a headache suddenly engulfs his brain.

"Look, it's kind of like we were doing you a favor really." He meets my eyes but the shadow in them betrays him. Even he doesn't believe what he's saying. "You're a lot safer now. Those rats you were with just want to steal other people's stuff."

"At least they're not stealing people. And what about Quinn? Do you think she's in danger right now?" I cross my arms across my chest. Does he really think he can justify his way out of this?

He releases a long sigh, as if I'm inconveniencing him with my questions.

"Quinn's tough. She can take care of herself. Who knows, maybe she's even made it home by now," he says, brimming with pride as if he'd just correctly answered a Final Jeopardy question.

Frustrated, I drop to the ground and pluck blades of grass from the soft dirt. So it's okay for me to leave my sister, but we can't even consider leaving his brother. Silence and shimmering air hover around us. There's no relief from the rising heat. Each layer seems to build off of the previous one.

I scramble deeper into the foliage, seeking reprieve. Propping up against a thick tree, I let my body meld into the trunk. A soft breeze stirs, fluttering wisps of hair across my neck. The comforting shade attempts to lull my eyes closed, but I'm not about to sleep on the ground. I mean, look where that got me last time.

Stretching to wake my muscles, I notice the sky. The bright sun has dulled since we stopped moving. Bright blue has morphed into a sickly yellow-green. My hair flaps around my face as the breeze kicks up. It's probably mid-afternoon, but it looks like the sky is mourning a precarious death.

"Dan!" I bark. He sits a few feet away from me, leaning

against another tree. He must have fallen asleep because he jumps at my outburst.

An inner voice practically screams in my ear. If you had just paid attention, you could have gotten away and he wouldn't have even noticed!

Dan rubs his eyes. "What is it, Riley?"

"Look at the sky! I think a storm's coming."

Aiming his bleary gaze upward, his eyes widen when they shoot to me. A gust of wind plows into both of us.

"Damn, I'd say you're right. Jim better get his ass back here soon."

Chapter 7

Thunder roars in the distance. The sky darkens with each passing minute. And our only protection is the towering evergreen we stand beneath.

"We need to find somewhere to go!" I plead. "We can't just stay out here." Again, I'm transported back to the car accident that ended my parents' lives. The rain. The smashing, crashing, crunching cars. I can't be out here in this.

"Jim'll be back any minute. We need to wait. He'll never find us if we move."

That thought provides a momentary distraction. I wouldn't exactly call that a bad thing.

"We'll be fine." Dan's tone confirms it's the end of the discussion.

The humid air enveloping my body does nothing to stop my chattering teeth. I stare at the clouds above in wonder and horror. They tumble and jostle as if waging war against each other. Dark streaks mar their formations, like sword slashes. Just how much longer do we have until they touch down?

A few minutes later, Jim rolls up. He balances on the bike, steering with one hand while grasping a small red gas can with the other.

"Get that bike upright! Let's fill it up and get the hell outta here," he shouts over the howling wind.

While the guys fumble with the bikes, I cautiously eye the sky. It's literally falling. Fuming clouds drift ever closer to the ground.

"Done!" Jim shouts, pulling me back to the scene. I dash over to Jim's bike, casting wary glances skyward. I'm ready to get out of here. I hop on the back and both bikes zoom away from our temporary shelter.

We race down the highway, swaying from one side to the other as wind gusts attempt to knock us off balance. When the first fat drops of rain pelt my skin, I know I'm at my breaking point.

Squeezing my eyes shut, I focus on forcing calmness through every muscle in my body, all the way to my trembling limbs, but it doesn't work.

Wind whips around me, plastering drenched tendrils of hair to my ears and neck. I don't dare let go of Jim to push them away.

Between the blustering wind, a sky that grows darker by the second, and the sheets of rain that plummet to the ground, we're completely exposed. How can Jim see to drive in this stuff? What if we slide? It's not like we have doors to protect our legs from the pavement.

"Jim!" I clutch his shirt, pulling it tight against his chest. "I. Can't. Stay. Out. Here." My searing voice implores him to understand. The last time I saw rain like this was when our car crashed, killing my parents. Anxiety courses through my veins, energizing each drop of blood in my body.

Without a response or even acknowledgement that he heard me, Jim's eyes remain fixed on the road ahead. I squeeze my eyes shut and focus on filling my lungs with the thick humid air, holding it for just a moment before pushing it out one tiny breath at a time.

A frustrated screech claws at the bottom of my throat, hungering to escape. Just as I clench my teeth in an attempt to quell the inevitable outburst, the bike decelerates. The breath I was holding rushes past my lips. My tense eyes relax into a squint.

With a swift hand motion, Jim gestures toward a clearing of trees.

I can barely make out a structure in the distance.

Dan pulls up alongside us, raising an arm in question.

Jim just repeats the gesture, wordlessly conveying our change in plans. Slowing the bike down to a crawl, Jim veers right off the highway.

As usual, Dan follows obediently.

We approach a white motorhome. The pouring rain blurs its red and gray decal swirls. The bikes slow; the engine sounds overpowered by sheets of precipitation.

Although we're just yards from the highway, the area feels remote. Other than the small dirt road we follow, green and brown blurs surround us. I'm not sure if it's because I can barely see anything in the torrential downpour or if we've happened upon a cluster of trees and shrubs. I'm just praying it's not a mirage my mind conjured in one last grasp for sanity.

The vibrating engine sputters and stills. I scramble to keep up as Jim hops off the bike and runs to the RV's door.

Seconds later, Dan joins him, pushing past me. Their muffled voices sound angry as they try to wrestle the locked door open.

Lightning shrieks across the sky, closely followed by erupting thunder. My eyes land on the smooth white side of the locked camper. Scrolling letters proudly designate this vehicle: The Land Stormer.

Before I realize what's happening, Jim seizes my arm and pushes me toward Dan, who rushes through the open door.

Chapter 8

Close on our heels, Jim sprints through the open door, slamming it shut behind him. We land in a slippery heap at the threshold. The chorus of our heavy breathing fills the otherwise empty motorhome.

Jim sits back on his haunches, raising a hand along the wall. A click sounds just before a soft glow illuminates the space. The lights work! I don't know how electricity works in an RV and I don't care—I'm just thrilled that we have some.

I sigh with relief as I contemplate the safety this RV promises. I've pushed through more emotions in the last seventeen days than I have in the last seventeen years.

We collect ourselves and stand, surveying our newfound shelter. It takes a few minutes for my lungs to step off the speed train, but once they do, I breathe a temporary sigh of relief. This place is pretty nice.

Plaid bucket seats await a driver and passenger at the front end. A large embroidered maroon "S" adorns the back of the driver's seat while a "J" in the same style labels the passenger's seat. A console juts up between the two, holding matching stainless-steel tumblers that sit in wait for their owners to return.

Toward the center of the interior, a tiny kitchen boasts wooden cupboards with a microwave built into them. A brown-and-white checkered towel dangles over the rim of the sink, nestled between a compact stove and fridge.

When Jim cautiously steps toward the driver's seat, I turn in the other direction. My muddied shoes imprint a trail along the tan vinyl floor as I mosey toward the back of the RV. It's a little late, but I notice a mat perched just past the door's threshold. I should probably wipe my shoes on it.

The brown mat features a black-outlined camper with a red heart on its door. Happy Campers is scrawled above the image and two names are scrawled below it: Steve & Jamie. It conveys the sense of happiness this place must bring them. I hope I can feel happiness again sometime soon.

I slowly open a narrow door that appears to lead to a closet. Instead, I'm greeted by a low-sitting toilet facing a rectangular shower stall. They're so close that I could probably wash my knees while doing my business. Not that I'd do that.

I spy a towel and soap by the tiny sink. Good to know we have options to improve our personal hygiene here.

Stepping out of the bathroom that's smaller than my closet back home, I explore a nook. Twin bunk beds offer a relaxing escape from the storm raging outside. In one fluid motion, I pull the moss green blanket down to reveal the sheets. Green and blue striped RVs dance along the tan background. I narrow my eyes at the words Happy Camper scrawled amongst the images.

We get it, Steve and Jamie, but I'm not here to camp and I'm not happy. Turning away from the ridiculous sheets, I search the small living room, which is really just the space between the kitchen and the bedroom. A worn blue loveseat sits across from a small television. Counting that, we technically have enough places to sleep if this storm holds up. There's no way I'm going back outside in this.

I return to the guys' conversation just as a gust of wind rocks the whole vehicle. My nerves tingle with remnants of the storm-induced adrenaline rush.

"It's good we found this place," Jim admits. "It's getting worse out there." He jabs a thumb toward the door. "Let's just hunker down here for the night. We can wake up early tomorrow and get back on the road."

That's probably the best thing I've ever heard Jim say. We've stopped, so at least I'm not moving farther away from my sister. And maybe sometime before tomorrow morning I can slip out of here.

Retreating to the bathroom, I hold my breath and turn the shower knob. Glorious water springs from it. I don't know how RVs work, but this one has running water, and I'm taking full advantage of it while I can.

After a long shower, I'm forced to put my grungy clothes back on. There's no way I'm walking out of this room wearing just a towel. I make a mental note to check the closets. Maybe Jamie has a spare shirt and shorts I can borrow? Okay, I probably won't be able to ever return any clothing I find, but it makes me feel better to pretend I will.

When I emerge from the bathroom, the guys are snooping through every closet, cupboard, and drawer they find. It's one thing to use this place for temporary shelter, but it feels wrong for them to be digging through someone else's belongings.

Dan notices me first. "Well, you look a lot better, Riley. A lot cleaner," he emphasizes.

Jim smacks his arm.

"Why don't you try and get some rest," Jim says, attempting to offer comfort.

With nothing else to do, I nod. I'm certainly not sleeping on the loveseat while they're still out there. I turn toward the closest bedroom and stride to the bunkbeds. Though lingering guilt slows my steps, I tiptoe toward the small chest of drawers. I was just thinking how bad it was for Dan and Jim to snoop through the RV, but I really want clean clothes.

Slowly pulling the top drawer open, I spy pastel-colored clothing. That's a good sign. The first folded shirt in the stack is a pale yellow. I carefully pull it from its place and hold it up as if I'm at a store trying to gauge if it'll fit without trying it on.

My smile collapses as gravity straightens the shirt in my hands. Oh, Jamie, why couldn't we be even somewhat close to the same size? The yellow shirt would make a better blanket on me. Quinn and I were always naturally thin, but the past week-and-a-half did anything but widen my frame.

When we were stranded at our Aunt Grace's trailer, we only ate when we remembered to. And, having spent most of each day hiding out in the trailer, we weren't burning much energy to work up any sort of appetite.

As I fold the too-large shirt and carefully return it to the drawer, I wonder where Quinn is right now. Maybe she's already in Pennsylvania. If she can just get home and get to our Aunt Robin, I know she'll be okay.

Even though I should be with Quinn right now, I pause for just one moment to marvel at our luck. We found shelter for the night. The last thing I want to do is hop on the back of Jim's bike just to get knocked around by the wind or drenched by the rain. I hope Quinn found some shelter, too.

In a strategic move, I take the lower bunk. If I can stay awake and the guys fall asleep, maybe I can tiptoe right out of here and never look back.

Chapter 9

Moments after I crawl into the lumpy bunk bed, my eyes drift closed while my mind wanders to places I can visit only in memories. Standing on the stage of my high school auditorium, the blinding spotlights blur my vision. When the music fades and the house lights surge to life, I scan the audience. A smile bursts across my face when I find my parents clapping wildly in the front row.

Confusion mars my features for a moment when I notice an empty seat next to my mom. Where's Quinn? She wouldn't miss one of my school plays. Mom and Dad would never let her skip it.

My best friend Stacy squeezes my hand, reminding me to bow in unison with our Footloose cast mates. Plastering a smile across my face, I follow the expected motions. After a round of applause, the curtains drift across the stage, encasing us in darkness for a moment.

As the stage lights slightly brighten, Stacy tugs me sideways. "Riley, what is up with you? Come on!" She guides me backstage. The usually bustling space is dim and deserted. Narrowing my eyes, I swivel my head back and forth, searching for costumed classmates.

"Where is everyone?" I ask. The only response is eerie silence. Turning in circles like a dog chasing its tail, I search for Stacy. But I'm alone. Completely alone.

Pushing past the navy-blue curtains, I rush through the auditorium door behind the stage. My legs stumble as my mind tries to comprehend why I'm surrounded by wood paneled walls.

Struggling to fill my lungs with air, I search my surroundings. I'd know this place anywhere. It's Aunt Grace's trailer. The place my family has visited for as many summers as I can remember. But no warm memories flash through my mind.

Instead, a tingling sensation races along my spine. My body propels forward, as if floating, down the short hallway. When I reach the open bedroom door, my mouth drops open in a silent scream.

Jim stands in the bedroom, shoulders hunched, face downcast. A shiny blade dangles from his left hand. Fresh crimson drops plop to the carpet as gravity guides them down. I catch his dark eyes just before mine land on the body curled up in a fetal position at his feet.

My knees crash to the floor, landing just out of reach of Quinn's lifeless form.

A heart-wrenching cry yanks me from the scene before I can reach my sister. My raw throat confirms that the scream must have clawed its way out of me. Turning my head side to side, I try to process the unfamiliar surroundings.

As my eyes adjust to the dark, the tan happy camper sheet zooms into focus. The words mock me. I'm stuck in this RV with Dan and Jim and I'm anything but happy.

A groggy voice from above asks, "Riley, was that you? Is everything okay?" I shakily answer, "It's just me, Dan. Sorry if I woke you." He must be in the top bunk. He grunts a wordless reply and settles back into his bed. Within minutes a gentle snoring reverberates through the space. Jim must be sleeping on the loveseat in the living room.

Wrapping myself in a tight hug, I let my thoughts drift to Quinn. I hope she's okay. She must have panicked when she woke up to find me gone. I wonder if she made it back home or if she went to the Dover base so she could be with Benny. I hope she's not wasting time looking for me.

I've got to get away from here. I can't believe this is even happening. Dan and Jim had no right to take me away from the only family I have left. But they made sure I understood that it was me or the others—and I couldn't let them hurt Quinn, or even Aidan, Jeff, Jasmine or Wes.

Determined to evade the path my thoughts are traveling down, I clench my eyes shut and will myself to stay awake. Once again, I've woken Dan, so I just need to wait until he falls back asleep. Then maybe I can get myself out of here.

Chapter 10

Of course, my ability to stay awake for more than a few minutes fails once more. So much for sneaking out under the cover of night.

When my body decides it's had enough sleep, my senses return in full force. A clanking sound echoes from the kitchenette. Dan yanks open each drawer and cabinet with the precision of Godzilla. Forks meet the floor faster than rain plummets to the ground lately.

Rising from the ruffled bed, I stretch, distancing myself from the happy camper sheets. When I wander toward the kitchen area, Dan greets me.

"Hey, Riley! I'm just taking inventory of our new supplies." He runs a calloused hand along the miniature kitchen cabinets. I nod in acknowledgement.

"How about some breakfast?" he asks cheerfully. It's just another day for him. Another day with his brother while I dangle in a continued loop of uncertainty. I don't even know if my sister is safe.

I flash a weak smile. "Find anything good?" I ask. Dan looks pleased with himself.

"Sure did! Jim, get in here and let's eat some breakfast. I found these big pouches of breakfast hash and scrambled eggs. You just add water and breakfast is ready."

"Sounds delicious," I say unenthusiastically. Dan shows off a small carton of orange juice before plopping three plastic cups on the counter and filling them.

We settle at the small table, eating in silence. The dehydrated food is surprisingly tasty. I feel like a prisoner who's eating her last meal. Gloom hangs heavy in the air. After swigging down the last drop of juice, Jim forcefully slams his cup on the table.

"What is it, Riley? I'm not spending this whole trip with you all moody." Oh really? Well, I didn't mean to upset him by letting my feelings show. Fine, if he wants to know, I'll tell him.

Unable to raise my head, I mutter. "Why, Jim? Why would you take me away from the only family I have left?" My voice cracks on the word family.

He huffs out a sharp breath in frustration. "You think you'd be better off with Quinn?" he barks.

"I'm her older sister, I should be taking care of her, making sure she's okay. Making sure she gets home." My words are soft but steady.

"She'll be just fine," he counters. "Quinn only cares about herself. People like that, they make it. They always find a way."

With those words, I level my eyes to meet his. I let them exude what I'm not brave enough to say. *Are you talking about Quinn right now? Or are you talking about yourself?*

Squeezing my eyes shut to hold back the hot tears threatening to fall, I mutter under my breath, "Then I guess you'll be just fine."

He either reads my mind or hears my utterance because fury swells in the air around us. Pressing both hands to his temples and clamping his eyes shut, he roars, "Because I never would have seen you again! I had to get outta there, and if you didn't come with me…" His eyes fly open in realization. He never meant for those words to be said.

Rescuing us both from the awkwardness, Dan stands and cautiously places a hand on his brother's shoulder. "Why don't you go blow off some steam?" Looking dazed, Jim shrugs off Dan's hand and strides out the door.

Once Jim's gone, Dan slowly sits down next to me. He stares into the distance for a few minutes before speaking.

"Riley, I'm sorry. We shouldn't have done this," Dan says quietly, slowly shaking his head. "You're no safer with us than you were with them. And Jim…he's not the same. It's just a matter of time before he snaps…again."

"What happened to him?" I whisper. "He wasn't always this cruel and controlling." I gulp, mentally cataloguing all the times Quinn pointed out Jim's bad points. "Was he?"

"After Dad died, he kinda decided he was in charge of everything," Dan says, flicking his eyes back and forth between the floor and me. His words are shaky, and I sense that he worries I won't believe him.

"Dan, what happened?" I gently rest my hand on his arm. "It's okay, you can tell me."

Water floods his eyes, but he manages to hold it there even when his words break. "Riley, we did some bad stuff." He shakes his head and runs a hand through his hair. "I think the reason Jim was so hell-bent on leaving was because he didn't wanna get caught."

I know what they did. They killed a neighbor at the trailer park and took her food. And I'm pretty sure they caught someone's cat and cooked it for dinner. But I'm not about to admit that right now. I'm certain Dan wasn't the driving force behind their vile actions.

I proceed cautiously. "What did you do?" Just how honest will he be with me?

Rolling his head back as if he's in physical pain, he confesses every evil they've committed over the past few weeks.

Chapter 11

When the Highway One pileup first happened, Dan and Jim used their dirt bikes to check out the scene. Not knowing what to do upon seeing the overwhelming devastation, they kind of freaked out when random crash survivors pleaded for help.

This led them to hide out at home for a few days. Not being prepared for an emergency situation, they had only so much food on hand.

"We never set out to hurt anyone," Dan says remorsefully. He avoids my eyes. "We started checking all the homes, to see which ones were empty and which had residents in them." They focused on the empty trailers—ransacking them for supplies.

One of the neighbors, Mrs. Adams, saw what they were doing. She confronted the guys, telling them she'd be calling the police as soon as the whole mess on the highway cleared up. Later that night, Jim went back to talk to Mrs. Adams, to try and convince her that they didn't do anything wrong.

The conversation went badly, and Jim's anger vaporized any shred of self-control that he had. Before even realizing it, he grabbed a knife from the kitchen and threatened her. She fled to the bedroom, trying to lock herself inside.

Jim gave chase and locked the door behind him, shutting Dan out.

"I heard her scream," he says, pressing a fist to his mouth. "I could tell they were struggling. He didn't mean to hurt her. He just…lost it…lost control of himself. Since Dad died, he flies off the handle over stupid stuff."

Kind of ironic the guys called Aidan and Jeff rats for doing the exact same thing: looking around the trailer park for supplies. Well, except they didn't hurt anyone in the process. In fact, Aidan and Jeff are the ones who warned us that we might not be safe at the trailer park. They found Mrs. Adams' body when they were searching what they thought was an empty home.

Dan continues, pulling my attention back to his explanation. The guys didn't speak about what happened. Instead, they stayed glued to the TV, watching the news. Jim grew more paranoid with each passing day, sure he'd get caught for murdering Mrs. Adams. When the survivors had been removed from the wreckage and a minimal path was cleared, they ventured back out to the highway. Scouting, watching for a chance to disappear.

When they did explore nearby towns, weaving between debris and highway damage on their road bikes, they didn't find many businesses open. At that point, they heard about Dover Air Force Base being open to civilians, but they didn't want to take a chance by staying that close. So they figured they'd go to

Langley Air Force Base. No one in Virginia would connect them to a random murder in Delaware. Especially with all the chaos along the East Coast.

Once they had a plan, Quinn and I stole their bikes. That one act changed the whole course of their plan. It didn't take long for the guys to figure out that we were acting funny the night their bikes disappeared. The only possible lead they could think of was Jeff and Aidan. At one point, Dan and Jim had seen the guys sneaking around the trailer park and followed them back to their temporary home base, a nearby campground. With no other possibilities, they had nothing to lose by following their hunch. After downing a few beers to spark their imagination, they formulated a plan to get their bikes back.

I take a few minutes of silence to process all that Dan's shared. He wears a pained expression from admitting to things that clearly bothered him, but I press my luck while the flood gates are open.

"Dan, why did you guys make me come with you?"

"Hell," he starts, heaving out a sigh. "Jim's been in love with you for years. I think he thought you'd be fine if he could just get you away from Quinn. You know, that maybe you felt the same way about him but couldn't show it in front of your sister."

My throat goes dry, forcing a gulp before any choked words will come out. The few bites of dehydrated eggs and potatoes I consumed are trying to climb their way back up my throat. Slowly shaking my head, I murmur, "But to not even give me a choice—"

A creaking door startles us both silent. Jim's back.

Chapter 12

Ignoring us, Jim slinks up to the front of the RV and roots around the dashboard and glove compartment.

My wide eyes meet Dan's and he whispers, "Don't say a word. I'm gonna get you outta here, Riley." With a pointer finger pressed to his lips, he makes a silent Shhh motion. Then, with one swift movement, he rises to his feet and starts toward his brother.

"Either of you see keys for this beast around here anywhere?" Jim calls out. Dan looks to me, but I just shake my head.

"No," Dan says. "What're you thinking?"

Jim turns toward me, as if I'm no longer invisible. Resting one arm on the driver's seat back, he smiles. "If we can get this thing running, why not take it the rest of the way? Sure beats the bikes. And if we run into any other weather, we can plow right through it."

"I think that's a great idea," Dan says a little too enthusiastically. I dumbly nod. While the RV does feel safe, definitely safer than the bikes, the last thing I want is to continue on this journey. I want to turn around right now and find Quinn. And, now that I know Dan is willing to help me, I'm even more anxious.

Jim drops to his knees and reaches under the seats. A smile spreads across his face as he retracts an arm and waves his prize in the air: a shiny silver key dangling from a black carabiner clip.

Inserting the key into the ignition, Jim gives us a confident smirk before twisting his wrist. The smirk disappears when the engine merely coughs out a low rattle.

"Dammit!" Jim bellows. "No wonder someone just left it here. Damn thing doesn't drive." I exhale a silent sigh of relief.

Dan approaches cautiously. "Do it again," he says. Annoyed, Jim shoots him a death glare before twisting the key again. It gives the same result.

Rubbing his chin, Dan wagers a guess. "You hear that faint clicking? It's tryin' to turn. Maybe we can just help it along." Turning the key one more time, Jim tilts his head toward the engine, staring in concentration. Removing the key, a grin splays across his face.

"You're right, brother," Jim says. "We may be in luck." As Jim and Dan scramble out the door and start tinkering under the hood, I decide to explore my temporary home. The owners don't seem to be coming back and if the guys can get this thing running, it'll be crossing state lines. I don't think Steve and Jamie will be seeing it again anytime soon.

Sifting through the kitchen cabinets and drawers, I find nothing interesting. Wandering up to the front of the RV again, my eyes run across the driver and passenger seats. What could be hiding up here?

Plopping into the passenger's seat, I explore the console rising from the carpeted floor. Typical goodies are stashed in the various compartments—sunglasses, sunscreen, a change purse crammed with coins, a tissue pack. Just as my fingers brush against a cold smooth object, the door creaks open. I jerk my hand back instinctively.

Jim appears, sliding into the driver's seat. "What're you doing?"

Adopting an innocent expression, I lean back into the bucket seat. "Just looking around. Kinda boring, you know?"

"Yeah, well you won't be bored much longer," he says proudly. "We almost got this thing fixed!" He inserts the key into the ignition and turns.

Good for them. They can get this thing fixed and drive it to the ends of the Earth for all I care. I just want to be free.

For a split-second it revs as if it'll start. But just as quickly, it emits a stale clicking noise.

"Dammit!" he barks. Shoulders slumped, he stomps back outside. Through the glass, I hear him and his brother arguing. Confident I have a few moments to myself, I reach back into the console, searching for my treasure.

When my fingers clasp the cold steel, a surge of power thrums through my body. Maybe I can take care of myself.

Chapter 13

Eyeing the knife's smooth black handle, I run a finger over the engraved monogram letters. SA. Must be Steve's. Wherever you are, Steve, thanks for leaving your knife behind.

Jerking my wrist, I flick the knife to free its blade. The worn edges and dings prove it's lived a past life or two. When the guys slam the hood down, my fumbling fingers close the knife and shove it into my shoe. That always seems to work on TV.

I jump to my feet just in time to greet Dan and Jim as they storm through the door. They charge right past me to the dashboard and jam the key into the ignition once more. This time, they erupt in congratulatory banter when the engine thrums to life. Jim revs the engine, and a loud roar announces that it's awakened.

"It was just some corroded battery terminals," Jim says proudly. "Easy fix. And look at that," he points toward the dashboard. "We got ourselves nearly a full tank of gas!"

My eyes nervously shift to Dan. When he catches my expression, realization surfaces.

"Hey Jim, what about the bikes? Should we try to load 'em up in here and take 'em with us? Or should we hide 'em in the woods in case we decide to come back?" He's stalling. He's still willing to help me get away. This just may work if he can keep Jim busy for a few minutes. I have never felt so thankful for Dan.

Jim scratches his chin. "We should probably hide them. I don't want to drag them in here and take up all the space." He lightly slaps Dan's chest. "Come on, we'll find someplace to put them for now…something we'll be able to find again if we need to." He throws me a sideways glance. "Don't want someone finding them and taking what's ours."

Quinn was right. He really is an ass. He plucked me right out of my life and he clearly has no guilt about that.

"We'll be back in a few minutes, Riley. Wanna see if there's anything left to eat? I'm hungry as hell." I guess he would be since he stomped off during breakfast.

"Sure, Jim." This is my chance. Dan's distracting Jim so I can get away. As soon as the door slams shut behind them, I race between the kitchen and bedroom. My eyes scan for anything useful. I snag a pouch of beef jerky and a can of V8 juice. It sounds disgusting, but if I'm desperate, it'll hold me over until I can do better. Dashing to the bedroom, I search the meager closet for a bag. I toss baseball caps and flip flops out of the way. No backpack, not even a flimsy plastic bag!

This is taking too long. I just need to go! As I throw the few items I've gathered onto the bed, the happy camper pillow beckons me. That's it! I yank the pillow free of its ridiculous case and toss my stolen belongings into it. Throwing it over my shoulder, I rush into the living room.

I fumble mid-step when the squeaky door shoots open. Nearly crying out in defeat, my eyes widen in horror. The faces before me are not Dan's and Jim's. I've never seen these people before, and they don't look friendly. I audibly gasp when three sets of eyes land on me.

Chapter 14

"Well, hello there," the middle guy says, smirking. "Is this your place?" Shifting on my feet, terror flashes through my veins.

"Well, um…" I don't know what to say. Work, brain, work!

"Or maybe you're just here playing house," another guy says, chuckling. Fear spikes along my spine. I struggle to draw in enough air. The walls seem to shift closer by the second. The already tight space is overtaken by these strangers.

The third guy looks nervously between me and the others. He pushes wire-rimmed glasses up the bridge of his nose.

"Guys, let's just go," he says meekly. Yeah, great idea. Listen to him!

"Now just hold up, Alex," the middle one says. He slicks his long dark hair back, out of his face. "I know I heard an engine start. And that's exactly what we need right now."

The second guy takes a step toward me, eyeing me like I'm a lost child and he's here to help. I guess he's taking a different approach.

"Hey, we didn't mean to scare you," he says. But you did and you're still doing it. He places a hand on his chest, directly over the pocket on his navy t-shirt. "I'm Hunter and this is Dylan and Alex." He points toward each in turn. He pauses, looking at me expectantly but I just stare at them mutely.

"Our ride kinda broke down and we need some wheels. We've been hiking on foot for about a day and we were nearby… thought we heard an engine start…so we came to check it out and see if we could maybe hitch a ride."

Shifting uncomfortably, I'm acutely aware of the knife hiding in my shoe. The handle shifts, jabbing into my arch. I almost laugh. Even if I felt confident enough to bend down and dig the knife from my shoe, my shaky hands would never be able to flick the blade out.

I open my mouth to respond but sound refuses to form. Muffled laughter invades the tense silence a moment before the squeaky door swings open again. I nearly crumple to the floor in relief.

Jim's eyes flutter over the scene before his face instantly transforms into a vicious snarl.

For a moment the only sound is the rapid beating of my heart as it races out of control.

"Who the hell are you?" he booms. I jump involuntarily, dropping the pillowcase of supplies I packed. The stupid V8 can tumbles out, rolling away until it bounces off the wall and sputters to a stop.

Hunter raises his hands in surrender. "Let's all calm down. We were just looking for some help."

Looking past all three strangers, Jim scrutinizes me. "You okay?" I nod quickly even though I'm anything but okay. He shifts his attention back to them.

"We don't have any help to give, so just be on your way. Now!" he says coldly. That earns him a smirk from the guy in the middle, who steps forward and makes introductions.

"Look, I'm Dylan and this is my brother Alex." He motions to the guy with glasses. "That's Hunter." He motions to the other guy. "So, is this thing yours?" he asks casually, waving his arms around the RV.

I slowly shuffle toward the wall. I need it for support. Tuning out the conversation, I evaluate my options. If I could just get out now, everyone would be distracted. The only problem? Dylan, Hunter, and Alex stand between me and the door. Their position also separates me from Dan and Jim.

Peering around my immediate surroundings, I search for ideas. The V8 can rests at my foot. Lot of good that's gonna do. Maybe if I had stronger arm muscles, I could hurl it at the guys and just shoot past them. I bet Quinn would try it. My heart aches when I think of her. But there's no time for that now.

The borrowed knife lies in wait in my shoe. If I try to grab it, I'll probably end up dropping it right at the strangers' feet. I just can't trust myself, and the last thing I want to do is give them a weapon. Dan and Jim are my only hope right now.

My head feels like it's caught in a vice and my vision blurs. Am I having a heart attack? How many times can my heart race in panic before it claims defeat? Rising tension, and voices, pull me back to the situation unfolding before me.

Before I know what's happening, Dylan lunges forward and wraps an arm around me. Just as fast, he whips a glinting blade out of his pocket and presses it to my cheek. A slice of warmth trickles down my face as I stifle a sob.

Chapter 15

My whole body trembles as my eyes well with tears. Before the scene blurs out of focus, a glint of fear flashes in Jim's dark eyes. Just as quickly, it shifts like quicksand into a layer of rage.

I'm such an idiot. I'm too busy getting lost inside my own head to fully pay attention to the threat standing just three feet away. This is not a world I belong in. Nowhere is truly safe anymore.

"What the hell do you think you're doing?" Jim snarls. Dylan huffs out a sharp laugh, his hot breath spreading over my neck. He eyes each of his friends, slightly turning my body along with his.

"I already told you what I'm doing," he says, focusing his attention back on Jim. "We want this RV, so you need to Get. The. Hell. Out."

His agitated voice amplifies in the small space. Claustrophobia claws at my throat and lungs. I close my eyes while I attempt to focus on slowing my breathing.

Fire erupts in my cheek as he drags the knife down an inch. An involuntary gasp escapes me, and tears spill full force, mingling with my blood to create a steady pink stream that deposits on my shirt.

My throat constricts, threatening to sever my oxygen lifeline. A chill sweeps through my limbs, numbing every inch except for the searing slice on my cheek. I should be with Quinn, not stuck in the middle of some stupid standoff.

"Dylan, man, let's just go," Alex says nervously. "We'll find something else." When he steps forward and places a hand on his brother's shoulder, the one I'm not pressed against, Dylan brushes him aside.

Although I can't see Dylan's face, the fire in his words sparks clearly. "No! Just shut up, Alex! I'm handling the sit—"

Before he can finish the thought, we're both knocked to the ground. As we fall the knife sears along my cheek, a burning sensation trailing its wake. The moment I land, a hand shoves me away. Instinctively, I tuck my head toward my chest as I roll.

As spots burst before my eyes I squint to focus on the unfolding scene. Jim and Dylan wrestle in a tangle of limbs, their grunts and profanity renting the air. Jim must have tackled Dylan while he was distracted. Blinking rapidly in an attempt to tame the stars shooting across my vision, I raise a hand to my right cheek.

Dan and the guy named Hunter are arguing, throwing their arms around. Their sounds are just vicious snarls. I can't make out the words. My head must have hit the floor harder than I thought.

Refocusing on Dylan and Jim, I see the other guy—Alex—trying to break up the fight. He takes more hits than he stops, but he stays at it. The guys are all practically on top of each other sandwiched between the sofa and dinette. I slink into the hallway, willing my body as far away from the ruckus as possible.

Among the fading bursts in my vision, a glint catches my eye. Locating the source, time slows as I see Jim grasp the knife that my blood still clings to.

I'm paralyzed with fear and fury. My watery eyes catch Jim's for a split second and I recognize his determination. He shoved me away and now he has to stop Dylan.

The scene pauses when Jim raises the knife behind his head. With the little bit of space left open from Jim's retreating arm, Alex attempts to wedge himself between the brawling bodies like a roadblock. He closes his eyes and inhales a deep breath in a silent victory. In that moment of eerie stillness Jim plunges the knife into unsuspecting flesh.

Chapter 16

Tears erupt from my eyes as the scene unfolds around me. Jim bounces up on his feet and wipes his mouth as he waits for the others to react. Dan and Hunter stand in stunned silence for a few beats.

Dylan reaches around Alex's quivering body, wrapping his hand around the hilt of the knife protruding from his brother's abdomen. In one smooth movement, he eases out from under Alex and gently rests his head on the floor.

"What did you do!" Dylan booms. He alternates between fury and concern. "Alex, can you hear me, man?" Alex watches Dylan, but his response is a choked gurgle. His eyes convey a hopeless panic, as if he's a fish flopping in the desert in search of nonexistent water.

Hunter rushes over to Alex's other side, silently conveying his concern to Dylan. As they turn to Jim, he thrusts an accusatory finger at them.

"Get out. Now!" he commands. "You should have left the first time I told you to."

While Hunter tends to Alex, Dylan jumps to his feet, taking a step toward Jim. "And what the hell are we supposed to do? You killed him. You see that? There's nowhere to get help out here. You killed him."

"I did what you were gonna do to us," Jim says with an eerie calm. "That knife was meant for you! It's not my fault he got in the damn way."

A gasp of pain pulls all of our attention to the floor. Hunter sits on his haunches over Alex. He holds the knife in his hand as Alex clamps a fist to the space previously occupied by the blade.

Dylan strides two steps over to them. "What the hell are you doing? You never remove a knife. Now he's gonna bleed even more!"

As the two argue over what to do, I see Jim motioning to Dan. Whatever Jim wants, Dan does not want any part of. He vigorously shakes his head in disagreement. Dylan continues to berate Hunter as Alex turns on his side, hunching his back as if he can will the slice on his stomach back together.

Dan must sense the rage radiating from Jim because he finally gives a defeated nod and turns his attention to the intruders. In one swift move, Dan rushes Hunter, swiping the knife out of his hand. Without missing a beat, he charges toward Jim, stopping short next to his brother.

My well of tears dries and the scene comes into sharper focus. I scramble in a backwards crab walk until I bump into the wall. Using it for support, I rise. I just want to disappear into the background.

The movement catches Jim's attention. "Riley, go wash up. You're bleeding all over the place." Raising a shaky hand to my cheek, my fingers land on viscous goo. Throwing Jim a quick nod, I'm relieved to be dismissed. I sway toward the bathroom on shaky legs.

With one last look before I escape the overwhelming tension, I catch Alex's eyes. My heart swells with sorrow. I've never seen life drain from someone but certainty sweeps over me. He's not going to recover from this injury. Alex's life force slithers further out of reach with each stream of blood flowing to the carpet.

Chapter 17

Shuddering, I rush to the bathroom. My trembling hands claw at the door. I rush inside, turn the lock and lean up against the flimsy barrier protecting me. After a moment, I swipe the closest towel. White, of course. Sorry, Steve and Jamie.

Leaning over the tiny sink, I turn the water on full blast. It does little to drown out the escalating voices a dozen feet away. I nearly jump out of my skin with every thud and thump.

Running the cloth under cold water, I dampen it and gently dab the gash, trying to clean it without inciting more blood. In a valiant distraction attempt, I inventory all the times I've done this sort of thing for Quinn. I'm not used to turning a healing hand on myself.

I was always the cautious one and Quinn made up for that tenfold. Whether she was getting her foot stuck in a bike or shoving a Barbie doll shoe up her nose, I was usually playing with her at the time, and thus the first one to act as a medic. A lopsided grin spreads across my face as my mind flashes through some of her most creative injuries.

After gently washing away the dried blood and wringing out the hand towel that's now spotted with pink stains, I prepare to investigate the sudden silence on the other side of the door. I don't even realize I'm wringing my hands until I have to separate them to unlock the door and turn the knob.

Quietly, I open the door a crack and peer into the living room. Dylan, Hunter, and Alex are gone. The only remnants of their presence are the deep red blotches marring the carpet. Steve and Jamie aren't going to appreciate that.

Dan and Jim speak in hushed tones as they attempt to cover the stains with blankets. They stop in their tracks when I emerge from the bathroom.

"Riley, you okay?" Dan asks, turning toward me.

Jim drops the blanket he's holding and takes slow, careful steps toward me as if I'm a cornered animal about to bolt.

My eyes volley back and forth between the guys as I try to steady my breathing. "A…are they gone? Are those guys gone now?" I look to the door and release a breath of relief when I see the lock latched.

"Riley, it's okay. It's all over now." A fresh trickle of blood rolls down my cheek. Without a word, I rush back to the bathroom. With a shaking hand, I press the towel against my check to stanch the blood. I pick through the tiny medicine cabinet but nothing useful sits on the narrow shelves. If I needed shaving cream, toothpaste, or eye drops, this would be a jackpot. Do Steve and Jamie not believe in first aid supplies?

"Hey!" Jim's voice outside the paper-thin door startles me. "You doing okay in there?"

"Yeah, I'm okay. Just cleaning up my face...again," I say dejectedly.

"Well as soon as you're done, we're gonna hightail it outta here. Now that this thing's running, we might as well get back on the road," he says through the door. A fresh wave of panic courses through every cell in my body.

No! We can't go. I'll never make it all the way back to the campground from Virginia. Maybe I can still get away if we stay here one more night. In a panic, I throw the door open, using my hysteria to my advantage for a change.

"No, please! I can't go anywhere!" I cry in a heaping mess of words. Shocked, Jim takes a step back. It's my cue to continue.

"Jim, please, let's just stay here one more night. I...I just... it's too much. Too much has happened, and I want to…just not think about going somewhere new right now," I allow my panic to overflow and await his response. The outburst draws Dan's attention and I feel his eyes watching me.

Jim scratches his head, shifting his attention back and forth between me and Dan. Tilting his head back and releasing a huff of breath, he exclaims a hearty, "Fine! But come morning, we're outta here."

I allow myself one deep breath. Somehow this small win is soothing. It's a small battle, but I won it! I swallow the smirk, attempting to declare my victory while Jim storms to the front of the RV. Dan narrows his eyes, silently questioning me. Maybe he can tell I was overreacting a bit. Maybe he knows that I'm trying to stall this trip in its tracks. He gives me a slight nod and opens his mouth to speak just as Jim calls for him.

"Dan, come here. We're gonna have to take turns keeping watch. In case those rats try to come back."

With one last glance, Dan closes his mouth and turns toward his brother. "Coming."

Chapter 18

While the guys discuss next steps, I return to the bathroom and finally convince my cheek to stop oozing. I take advantage of the toothpaste in the medicine cabinet and use my finger as a makeshift toothbrush.

With nothing else to do, I open the bathroom door. Jim and Dan stand in the cramped living room as if they were waiting for me. Jim's tone and expression have softened.

"How's that cheek?" he asks.

"It's okay. It finally stopped bleeding at least," I answer honestly. I think what hurt more was the act of it. The fact that someone could so easily hurt me, intentionally. And that I was helpless to defend myself or prevent it from happening in the first place.

"Riley, you should get some rest. Dan's gonna take first watch." Turning toward his brother, he continues. "If anyone comes around here, you get me right away," Jim commands. Dan gives a salute and turns toward the door. He pauses when his eyes scan the kitchen.

"Any beers in there? I could sure use one tonight," Dan says, smirking, motioning toward the compact fridge. Jim's not amused.

"Don't worry about that right now! You gotta stay sharp. Now go on outside and take watch." Without another word, Dan steps to the door and exits the RV.

I turn away and slog toward the bedroom. While my feet are slow, my mind races. I can sneak out if I just wait until the guys fall asleep. Dan can't stay awake all night. My mind teases running away in the night, finding my way back to the campground.

Well, that's if Quinn is still there. I push away thoughts of her waking up to find me gone. If she stayed with the group, she may be headed in the same direction as us.

I'm startled when Jim wraps a strong arm around my waist. Guiding me to the bottom bunk, he yanks down the blankets and turns to face me. "Just try to forget about tonight, okay? They're gone and they ain't coming back." He motions for me to lie down. Kicking off my shoes, I climb onto the bed and let him pull the covers up to my chin.

"It's all right now, Riley. You're safe here with us."

He hovers for a moment, watching me, but I stay silent. Letting my eyes drift closed, I allow his words to wrap me in a blanket of security. Since my life split at the seams, all I've wanted is to feel safe. And to have my family back. At this one moment in time, feeling safe, even if it's just for a short time, sounds pretty good.

As soon as Jim's footsteps fade from the room, I force my eyes back open with a sharp command for my brain to stay awake. Quinn always said my superpower was sleeping. I can fall asleep virtually anywhere and sleep through almost anything. Right about now I'd give anything for a splash of insomnia. If I can just stay awake until Jim falls asleep, I'll have no problem getting away. Even if Dan's on watch, I know he'll help me.

I start planning my latest escape attempt, but after a few minutes, I sink deeper into the mattress in defeat. The odds are stacked against me. Even if the squeaky door doesn't sound the alarm on my escape, even if Jim didn't try to find me, and even if I could find my way back to the campground, there's no guarantee Quinn is still there.

Lying on my side, I stare into the RV's kitchen area. The thin blanket and squishy pillow invite me to shut the world out. Jim showers in the tiny bathroom, the hum of streaming water lulling my eyes to drift closed.

Nowhere is safe. I can't just run off by myself and expect to find my sister. She could be anywhere. And she's not the only one out there. People like Dylan and Hunter lurk, and not just in shadows and corners.

The last thing I see before my eyelids meet is Dan sneaking into the refrigerator and swiping a six-pack of beer before he high-tails it back outside.

Once again, I lose the battle to stay awake. I must sleep for hours because when my senses start to awaken, daylight streams into the RV. Even with my eyes still closed, I can tell it's morning and I've missed another chance to sneak away.

I start to stretch my muscles but jolt into a constricted posture when an agonized scream punctures the air. My unfocused eyes widen when Jim throws open the RV's door, staggering through it. He's half-carrying Dan and attempts to lower his brother onto the kitchen table. Stumbling to my feet, I launch myself toward the guys.

"Dammit, Dan, hold still!" Jim hisses. No part of Dan is calm or still. His whole body convulses as a swarm of tiny red-brown bodies flow over his skin like a dancing river.

Chapter 19

My hands fly to my face, covering my gaping mouth. No. I can't be seeing this. This can't be happening. He writhes on the table, twisting as if to escape his own skin. Jim hovers over him, swiping the swift-moving insects away from Dan's exposed arms and face.

Memories flood back to when I was six and we discovered I was allergic to bee stings. A gulp of air catches in my throat as I recall the constricting vice my throat became, making it hard to swallow or speak. The burning, the swelling. Dan looks like he's been stung by the furious residents of a massive hive.

Except these bugs have no wings. Their little legs carry them over Dan's body faster than a roller coaster plunges down a steep hill. It's as if an ant hill has erupted on his chest and little soldiers evacuate in all directions.

Throwing a glance my way, Jim belts out orders. "Riley! Open the shower door! Turn the water on!"

I force my shaky legs to act. Scrambling to the tiny bathroom, I burst into the shower and twist the knob. Icy water blasts through the stall. I back away and sidle out of the bathroom.

"Help me lift him!" Jim shouts.

I stumble to the table and grab Dan's left shoulder, hoisting him up in tandem with Jim.

"We're gonna try to wash all this shit off him," Jim commands.

Like a small gang of drunks, we clumsily sway toward the tiny bathroom. There's no way we can all fit in the miniscule space. Jim must realize this as we crest the threshold because he angles himself through the doorway first, pivoting Dan around himself and into the cleansing stream of water.

An idea bursting to life in my head, I run to the kitchen, yanking every door and cupboard open. There must be a first aid kit here somewhere. We just didn't look hard enough. And something is seriously wrong with Steve and Jamie if they're traipsing all around the country without even one skimpy cotton ball or band aid.

I yank open the closet door in the living room area. My eyes track along the narrow shelves, silently inventorying each item: towels, sunscreen, bug-spray. Nothing that can help us right now. Once again, this faceless couple has let me down.

"Riley! Where the hell are you?" Jim roars. "Find some towels or something and help me get him out of here!"

Ignoring the harshness in his words, I yank a towel off the closest shelf and dart toward the bathroom.

Both Jim and Dan are a sopping mess. I help boost Dan's limp body as we make our way toward the master bedroom. Gently we lower Dan to the bed and I towel off the parts of his skin that look normal.

Although he remains silent, Dan's eyes drip with misery. His face is contorted in a mask of pain. The silence breaks when I gently dab one of the open sores on his neck.

"Ooooowwww," he shouts, throwing his damaged arms up to protect his neck. I back away and examine his injuries. His hands, arms, neck and face are marred with dozens of angry red bumps. Some bulge with white bubbles.

Jim steps beside me, a towel wrapped around his shoulders. He must have found the closet stash and dried off. He rubs his forehead, staring at his brother.

A shriek of thunder startles all of us. "Another damn storm!" Jim booms. "What the hell's going on?"

I hunch my shoulders in reply. Wind blasts the exterior, emitting a low howl. Lightning flashes through the windows. An involuntary shudder courses through my body. This storm isn't the only thing lurking outside the RV's walls.

If those guys come back, they could sneak up on us at any time. Dan's in no shape to help guard the place and I certainly can't protect us. I couldn't even manage to stay in a campground for one night without being abducted.

The lights flicker for a moment and I meet Jim's worried eyes. Please don't let us lose power. Shallow breathing pulls my attention back to the bed. Dan's body begins convulsing. This was just a temporary breather. A sinking feeling in my gut promises that this is about to get worse.

Chapter 20

Running a hand across his stubbly chin, Jim sweeps his gaze over me and Dan. His eyes betray exactly what he sees in us right now. Weakness. He heaves out a deep breath. As if that cleared his mind, he's suddenly focused. He's always got a plan, doesn't he?

"Look around in the closet and cabinets. Try to find some lotion, like calamine or something you'd put on a sunburn." When I don't respond, his voice rises. "Come on, Riley, snap out of it! I need your help!"

I rush around, yanking on drawers and cupboards, knocking shampoo bottles and mouthwash out of the way in my search.

Rain pelts the roof. I ignore it. We've got bigger problems right now.

In the middle of everything happening inside the RV, the storm raging outside is just a nuisance added on to our growing list of issues. A shriek of thunder lances the atmosphere. The only way this could be any worse is if Dylan still had a knife pressed into my skin. But compared to Alex, I'm lucky. I wouldn't wish what happened to him on anyone.

"I'm not finding anything!" I shout. Dan will be okay. If I just repeat it enough times, maybe it'll be true.

"I got an idea," Jim hollers. "Get a bunch of towels wet, use cold water. We'll use 'em like a compress on his skin." He huffs out a breath that's half desperation, half resignation.

I fumble through the closet, grabbing a stack of clean towels. Pushing my tired muscles, I rush to the bathroom and throw the towels in the sink one at a time. With each rush of cold water, I drown a towel, twist it out and toss it to Jim.

He immediately applies each one to his brother's exposed skin.

Dan whimpers with each touch, but once we're finished, he settles into the bed, a mound of wet cotton soothing his sores.

Jim's voice drifts to my ears. He mutters to himself, thinking out loud. "We're not gonna make it too far like this." He scratches his head, debating with himself. "Vic's place isn't too far from here…he's probably taken off somewhere…swing by, get Dan patched up, maybe find some clean clothes,…get back on the road." He starts walking toward the driver's seat. Fire boils in the pit of my stomach. He's not even going to bother telling me the plan.

Frustration, fear, and fatigue flare within me, erupting in my words. "Hey!" I shout, instantly surprised by my bold tone. Stopping mid-step, he turns toward me, eyebrows raised. Good. I have his attention.

"What's going on? What are we doing? What are you planning?" The questions spill out of my mouth as fast as my mind can form them. They sound more like demands than questions, though. Masking a momentary flash of annoyance, Jim slowly steps toward me and reaches out to touch my shoulder.

"Now just calm down," he starts.

"No! I will not calm down! You brought me with you against my will and now you're taking me somewhere and you won't say where." I border on pushing further but a nervous twinge in my belly signals a warning. I've seen Jim when he's angry and I don't really want to be on the receiving end of it.

Turning his head sideways like a confused dog, he hesitates before responding.

"Alright, Riley, here's the deal." He watches me closely as if I'm on the verge of sprouting another head. "I got a friend who lives around here, maybe ten or so miles away. Since everyone seems to have damn near disappeared, he's probably gone too. We'll just swing by and borrow some supplies. He'll never even know we were there. We need a solid first aid kit to patch Dan up. And you could use something for your face."

Running his eyes down my body he adds, "And we've got to get you a change of clothes. You can't walk into a military base looking like that. They'll think you're some kind of serial killer or something."

Meeting his eyes in a rare moment of bravery, I reply. "Isn't that ironic when I'm probably the only one here who's never killed anyone." With that, I turn on my heel and march to Dan's side.

Though I don't look back, I can feel Jim's eyes on me. Thank goodness he doesn't have laser vision. I'd be toast by now. Heavy footsteps stomp toward the front of the RV. As he settles into the driver's seat, he adjusts the mirrors and tosses aside anything that gets in his way.

When I reach Dan's side, his hitched breathing hangs in the air. His swollen eyes are pressed closed. Hushed moans slip from his lips every few seconds. Those bugs looked like fire ants. I've seen them before, but I've never been stung by one, let alone the hundreds that were crawling on him. If he has enough poison in his body, he could go into shock.

With Dan resting, if you can even call it that, I make my way to the passenger's seat. Jim's driving is slow and cautious. As anxious as he is to try and get help, at least he knows not to bounce Dan around or risk sliding on the wet roads.

As I slip into the bucket seat, Jim's dark eyes wash over me. "How is he?"

"He looks like he's trying to sleep," I say honestly. The adrenaline rush from my brief stand has passed. Now I'm back to worrying about Dan. "But I think those were fire ants swarming all over him. And if that's what they were, that means he's full of their poison."

Rubbing his forehead, Jim agrees with me. "I think you're right. I've never seen so many damn ants."

"I couldn't find any lotion or anything that I think would help him. Maybe the people who own this RV took the first aid kit with them. I mean, don't you think we would have found something useful by now?"

Keeping his eyes on the road, he easily maneuvers down the highway. Thankfully, this storm lacks the wind gusts the last one had. It seems like the farther south we go, the clearer the roads are and the easier they are to navigate.

"He's suffering and we don't know what the hell to do about it," Jim sighs. "We have no medical supplies. No medical experience." I sit in silence. For once I agree with Jim. I'm used to feeling helpless, but this must be a new emotion for him.

"If we can't find help, we may have to do the only thing we can for him," he continues. Narrowing my eyes, I watch his face for clues. He can't possibly be saying that he'd put Dan out of his misery if it came to that, is he?

"You can see how much pain he's in right now. He can't even talk. It's like he's being tortured in his own body," Jim says quietly. "I'd want the same thing if that happened to me. And I would do that for you too, Riley. I wouldn't let you suffer like that. No way."

Chapter 21

Iclose my eyes in morbid comprehension and swallow the bile rising in my throat. So if I got hurt and he couldn't help me, he'd just decide when I had enough? And I'd have no say in the matter? His thoughts swing from one extreme to the other. His first thought when he saw Dylan, Hunter, and Alex in the RV was to ask if I was okay. And now he's saying he'd put me out of my misery if it came to that?

A chill rushes from my core to my fingertips. Numb. Every part of me feels numb. I can't accept Jim's way of thinking. I know we can get Dan help. And I would be haunted for the rest of my life if we gave up on him now.

Anguish unfolds within every cell of my body, grasping each corner of my brain. What if Jim's friend won't help us? I can't lose Dan. And I can't face Jim alone.

"Riley," Jim calmly explains, as if it's an inconvenience. "I only do what I have to do. To protect us." He motions between me and him. "Whatever it takes to keep us safe."

My stomach recoils at the mention of "us." Jim and I are not an "us" and we never will be.

Failing miserably at holding a steady voice, I ask, "And what about Quinn? Who's keeping her safe?" All calm leaves his face as his features scrunch in anger.

"Your sister is fine! You need to get her out of your head." His voice rises with each word. And here we go again with the mood shifts. Dan's words come to mind, "He flies off the handle over stupid stuff."

Mindlessly, I nod.

The flood of emotions recedes. His beady eyes flash relief.

I almost release a maniacal giggle. Beady is a word Quinn would use to describe his soulless eyes. Quinn. I stare straight ahead as we continue down the road. Memories of my younger sister dance through my head. The swing set we spent hours playing on in the summers. The elaborate scenarios we'd imagine for our Barbie dolls. Arguing over whose turn it was to hold the leash when we took Snickers, our family dog, for a walk.

My nose burns as I stifle the tears that fight for release. This is not the Jim I grew up with. And really, we only saw him and his brother during vacations. It's not like we were next-door neighbors and saw each other every day.

I never believed Jim could do the things he's done. I always thought Quinn was rude to him, but maybe she saw what I couldn't, and I didn't trust her instincts.

My wandering thoughts shift into steely resolve. I now know

what Jim is capable of. And I will not let Quinn be his next victim. I was the older sister but only chronologically. Quinn was always braver, bolder, and more assertive. She doesn't know it, but at this moment I am finally claiming the role I should have taken the day she was born. I will protect her the only way I can. By keeping Jim far away from her.

Chapter 22

We drive in silence for about ten minutes, moving farther away from civilization with each passing second. After a few turns, the rolling hills look more like a construction site. Upturned dirt and giant tubes line an enormous ditch.

"What's all this?" I ask, my face pressed to the window.

"Pipeline. They started it weeks ago," Jim answers absently. "Looks like they're taking a break or maybe they put the whole damn thing on hold." He mutters to himself, "Probably not safe with all this crazy weather lately."

Just past where the construction stops, Jim turns onto a small dirt road. Dust kicks up, clouding around the RV. When stones start pinging off the tires, Jim slows to a crawl. The driveway's gotta be about a mile long, it winds around small buildings that look like storage sheds.

Since we're barely moving, I unbuckle the seatbelt and shuffle to the back to check on Dan. His eyes are open, but they're still slits. His whole face is a swollen red blotch. He must sense me or maybe my shadow crossed his narrow field of vision.

"We there yet?" he asks hopefully. "We at the base?" His voice is scratchy.

"Not yet," I say as pleasantly as possible. "But we're going to get there soon. We're just making one stop to try and get you some medicine, okay?"

He lets out a disappointed huff.

Jim shifts the RV into park and hops out of the driver's seat. He crowds in next to me.

"You alright, Dan?" He shoots me a worried glance. I doubt Dan can see that kind of detail right now.

Dan slowly shakes his head. "I need...a doctor...or a hospital. Something."

"You hang on," Jim says. "Just a little longer, brother, and you're gonna be okay." With that, Jim stands, turns on his heel, and strides toward the door.

I follow. Besides anything we can borrow to help Dan, we're also hoping to get a change of clothes for me. Dried blood stains don't coincide with the impression I want to make when trying to enter a military base.

Jim throws the door open, revealing a sprawling white colonial-style house. My eyes wander across the never-ending yard. I would expect a perfectly manicured lawn and maybe an in-ground pool or gazebo to accompany the spacious home, but instead I see dogs. Dozens of dogs.

You'd never know these pups were back here. They're

completely hidden from the road, along with the scattering of downtrodden doghouses. Some are barrels resting on their sides with a square opening cut into the round lid. Others are wooden boxes with worn roofs. Their circular dirt spaces are just inches apart, though not close enough that the dogs can reach each other.

They remind me of our family dog, Snickers. We left him at our aunt's house when we left for vacation. He's probably still there. Wondering why we aren't coming back.

My feet shuffle toward the dogs. I need a closer look. And I can tell they'd like one too.

I'm not sure how many eyes stalk me but the sensation of being under a microscope creeps up my neck. They watch our every move. A few snarl but most just stare intently.

"J-Jim," I nervously stutter. "What is this place?" His glare shifts from the dogs to me.

"It's just a…friend's place," he answers impatiently.

"Well, they don't look very happy," I note. "Why are they all chained out here? Are there more inside?"

"No, he keeps them all out here," he says dryly. "Look, why don't you go back to the RV and wait there. I'm just gonna run inside, grab what we need, and then we're gonna get the hell out of here."

"But I thought we were supposed to try and get some clean clothes for me. I should probably be there for that to see what would fit," I protest. What kind of person lives here?

"Just wait in the RV," he snaps. "If I can get you any clothes, I will. And I'll bring them out to you. Now go."

"I want to know what this place is!" Even I'm surprised by

my tone. I'm tired of feeling like the world is upside down and inside out. Everything is wrong. And there's no guarantee that it will ever be right again.

Jim sighs, scratching his chin. "It's kind of a place to gamble," he says quietly.

Crossing my arms, I prod. "Gamble on what?"

"The dogs, Riley. It's a dogfighting ring."

My stomach lurches and tears spring to my eyes. Those dogs aren't pets. They're captives. Forced to fight for their lives so people like Jim can win money.

"Look, Riley, I know it seems—"

"No! I really don't want to hear any more! Nothing you can say would ever justify forcing those poor animals to fight!" As far as I'm concerned, Jim and his stupid friend are worse than Dylan. At least with people like that, you can try to reason and try to defend yourself. Those poor dogs are at the mercy of cruel humans.

Without another word, I turn on my heel and stomp back toward the driveway. As I pass one of the zillion sheds on the property, a muffled bark stops me mid-step. Pressing my face and hands to the dusty window, I peer inside. The source of the bark watches me with curious interest.

What I assume is a mama dog lays in the shed, surrounded by five squirming puppies. She attempts to clean their brown and white coats while they playfully nip at each other. The dopey smile overtaking my face quickly falters. These adorable babies were born to fight, just like the others. They have no idea the horrific future that awaits them.

In that moment a fire flickers in my bones. I'm going to

change their future. If I can just figure out how to change my own first.

Chapter 23

This place reeks of violence and despair. Why would anyone come here? Shouting from the house startles me. Sounds like Jim's friend is home and isn't very interested in helping us. That's just fine with me. I don't think I really want help from someone who keeps all these dogs chained up like prisoners.

My anger fuels bravery. I don't need to stay with Jim just to keep him away from Quinn. I have a choice and I will not let him control my fate. I could do it. Right now. I could just run and run until my legs scream with pain. I could pretend I'm Quinn competing in a track meet, except the prize is freedom and the finish line is home.

Thinking of Dan, my resolve wanes. If I leave, will Jim do everything he can to get Dan to the base? Or will he just as soon give up? I can't take that chance. No matter what happened, Dan doesn't deserve that. And, even if Jim did keep going, what if they run into more trouble? Jim can't fight off every bad guy, dodge the weather and take care of Dan at the same time.

Slowly spinning 360 degrees, I take in every detail of my surroundings, including the address on the mailbox: 74 Newport Lane.

Thinking of the ride here, I remember the pipeline project. That's a huge landmark. It will guide me back. I lock eyes with the mama dog, making her a silent promise.

With a sense of purpose, I charge into the RV. I know exactly what I need. Digging into the console, my fingers scramble for the perfectly folded rectangle I'd spotted earlier. A smile passes over my face when I unfold the street map and pinpoint the location. Reaching into another compartment, I snag the blue ballpoint pen I saw earlier. Thank you, Steve and Jamie.

Carefully folding the map a few sizes smaller than its original shape, I shove it into my back pocket. No matter where I end up, it's coming with me.

Feeling a slight sense of accomplishment, I decide to fulfill my original mission and check on Dan. His eyes remain closed, but his fitful movements confirm he's not really resting. It's like his body can't stay still.

Since he's not even cognizant that I'm here, I wander back to the passenger's seat and wait patiently for Jim to return. Before long, a figure dashes around the RV and throws open the door. Jim rushes to the driver's seat and starts the engine.

I just stare. He's got no clothes for me, no supplies. Nothing. I believe that unfamiliar look in his eyes is fear. More shouting erupts outside the RV as Jim tears down the driveway, as if he can't get far enough away from this place fast enough.

Scrambling to buckle myself in, I demand, "What happened?" I'm still angry that Jim would even associate with a place like that.

Running a hand through his hair and releasing a deep breath, Jim answers quietly. "Vic's home and he's not gonna help us. And let's just say he wasn't too happy that I showed up here."

Smugly crossing my arms, I say, "That's surprising. The monster who forces dogs to fight for their lives didn't want to give us a hand."

"Alright, Riley, that's enough. Look, I know he's an ass and he does shitty things, okay? Don't worry, I won't be going there anymore." Patting the map hiding in my pocket I keep my thoughts to myself. Maybe you won't be back there, but I will be paying Vic a visit if it's the last thing I do.

Chapter 24

As we proceed farther south, the ride is mostly quiet. The only sounds are Dan's occasional moans. After about thirty minutes of driving, we come upon a town unlike any other place we've passed through. It's abuzz with life.

Emergency vehicles are strategically placed every few blocks. Uniformed firefighters and police direct people in long lines as if they're in chutes. Most are on foot, trudging along. Worry and luggage weigh them down and slow their steps.

We drive at a snail's pace, taking in the scene. A particularly gruff-looking firefighter stalks down the street, hanging white posters on telephone poles. Large black print instructs residents to seek shelter at designated local "safe zones." That must be where the emergency personnel are directing people.

I glance at Jim. If we go to a shelter, maybe I can find someone to help me. I can just explain that Jim forced me to come with him and I just want to go home. Even if I had to stay here for a little while, at least I wouldn't be heading farther away from Quinn anymore.

Temporary signs spring up along the side of the road that read: Bridge Closed Ahead. Worry lines etch Jim's forehead. An older man wearing a reflective Fire Police jacket waves us down. We slow to a stop and Jim lowers his window.

"You gotta turn back," the man says. "This road leads to the bridge and it's closed."

"We just want to cross over it and be on our way," Jim explains. "Looks fine to me," he adds under his breath.

The man's bushy white eyebrows shoot up. "The city says it isn't structurally sound. You know, since the aftershocks hit." He waves a hand in the air as if he's not entirely convinced the bridge needs to be closed. "Some kind of engineers have to test it and make sure it's safe. Until then, it's closed. Now follow me, I'll show you where you can park that thing and we'll get you to the safe zone."

This time my eyebrows jump. *We're going to the safe zone?* Relief courses through me. This road trip is over.

"Alright, sir," Jim complies. "I'll just turn around at the end of the street and come back." The man nods his head and turns his attention back to the crowd of people being directed down the street.

We slowly roll along the road. Jim swerves wide to make the turn, hesitating for a moment. Shooting me a determined look, he mutters, "Hold on."

Without another thought, he pounds the gas pedal to the floor. In a sports car, that may have some impact, but in this giant box on wheels, the RV barely chugs to life. Still, my heart races when screaming voices outside command us to stop.

"It's closed! We aren't allowed on it!" I screech, my words vying for attention over the struggling engine. We just got this thing working and he wants to push it to its limits?

"We're not going to their little "safe zone." We're getting to that base, where they can help Dan! And I'll be damned if we're taking the long way around because these yahoos think they own the bridge!" His eyes don't leave the road. Nothing I say will stop him.

Sirens blare behind us. He's going to get us arrested. That might finally be my way out, I realize.

We blast past the "Bridge Closed" sign and venture across the massive structure. The rearview mirror lights up, reflecting red and blue flashing lights. Emergency vehicles wait at the ready, hovering just before the invisible barrier between the road and the bridge.

"They're not coming!" Jim shouts, punching the dashboard with his fist. "Those chicken shits." He shoots me a satisfied smile.

"Maybe they know more about this bridge than we do!" I shout. It's a long drop to that murky water below. Fear twists in my gut. I grasp the door handle so tightly my knuckles bulge. A ghost of the rushing cold water washes over me and my skin erupts with goosebumps.

Slight vibrations rock the RV, replacing the smile on Jim's face with concern. His eyes widen as he grips the steering wheel tighter. When the vibrations get stronger, his face pales to match his straining knuckles.

We barrel toward the safety of land on the other side of the bridge. Just as we pass the midway point, a loud crack assaults the atmosphere. The concrete. The concrete beneath us is cracking. Maybe it was already cracked, and the weight of the RV was just enough to pry it open?

"This damn thing won't go any faster!" Jim panics. Sweat beads on his forehead, prompting me to say a silent prayer.

Please don't let Jim's sweaty forehead be the last thing I see before I die. Memories flash through my mind: family picnics and reunions, meeting our dog at the animal shelter, cheering on Quinn at track meets. Tension spikes as we race to solid ground. With just a few yards to go, a metallic screeching threatens to burst my eardrums. I press my palms over them, which does nothing to muffle the horrid sound.

Dan calls out, "What's happening?"

I glance toward the rear of the RV. Dan is clutching his head as if each sound drives a spear deeper into his skull.

"It's okay," Jim yells back in a flat tone.

Nothing is okay, my brain screams. Maybe he's just trying to act calm for Dan's benefit.

"Just a…little…traffic…issue." He glances my way as if to say, 'keep quiet.' "But we're gonna get the hell outta here—one way or another."

Moments after we reach the other side, the bridge tumbles into the swirling water below. The world is literally falling apart around us. It doesn't matter where we go or what we do. Nowhere is safe anymore.

The RV blasts through the warning signs on the other side attempting to block access to the bridge. The force hurls construction barrels and orange-and-white-striped bars through the air. They land with clunks and clangs along the shoulder.

Thankfully, there aren't any emergency vehicles lining this side. Maybe the people here already evacuated? Either way, we've just created one more emergency situation to stack on top of the previous ones.

Chapter 25

We drive in silence for nearly an hour. Every now and then Jim throws out a comment, but I don't reply. "We're down to a quarter tank of gas now, I hope we make it there soon." And eventually a "Check it out, Riley, we just passed the state line, we're in Virginia."

I guess I should be happy that we made it this far, but I can't help but focus on the scars we've picked up along the way. Pain flares in my cheek when I absentmindedly rest my face on my balled-up fist. And my wound is nothing compared to Dan's bite-covered body.

I glance back at Dan as we drive. His body twitches and I'm praying it's just restless sleep. He may be drifting in and out of consciousness for all I know. At this point, I may have exceeded my lifetime's allotment of worry. The only way I can survive this situation is to numb my mind.

"Riley, why don't you head back to the bathroom, wash up your face one more time," he says softly. "It doesn't look bad, but just in case there's any dried blood over your scar, you know… might be good to check."

Without a word, I unbuckle myself and march to the bathroom. The mirror reflects a tired, worn soul. I almost forgot about the dried blood stains on my shirt. With no better idea, I take it off and turn it inside out. Pulling it back on, the stains are a little less pronounced. I make a mental note to start wearing more maroon.

Although the seams show along the sides and sleeves, my hair easily covers the tag. Not great, but better.

Finding a clean washcloth, I dab my scar, cleaning it as best I can. Remnants of dried blood vanish but an angry red line remains. Oh well, nothing I can do about that right now.

When we reach Newport News, Jim insists that we start planning what we'll tell people at the base. I have nothing to discuss. I shouldn't even be here. But he has plenty of words for me.

"So, Riley," he starts, nervously glancing over trying to gauge my reaction. I stare straight ahead, my face an emotionless mask. He seems nervous, although I have no idea why. He's had the upper hand ever since he snatched me from the campground.

Why did he wait until the last minute to talk about this? I wonder if he thought, by now, I'd be okay with everything and I'd just go along with it. Maybe he's right. What little fight I ever had in me has dissipated.

"We're gonna need a story to tell them at the base. You know, so they let us in and keep us together," he says.

A brief flash of humor subsides before my body can release an inappropriate giggle. Together—with you? Yeah, that's about the last place I want to be. My eyes remain focused on the road.

We're definitely almost there. Street signs direct us to our destination. A few miles later, a rectangular tan slab rises from a brick platform. Its black block letters welcome us to Langley Air Force Base. We made it, and I'm a hundred miles away from my sister. I may never see her again.

Jim takes my silence as an invitation to continue speaking.

"So, Riley, I'll do all the talking for us," he says. "You just nod and look like you agree with everything I say." Whatever. I can't be with Quinn, but at least I know she's safe from Jim. That knowledge fills a tiny gap in my heart with solace.

Jim slowly rolls the RV along the road. As we near the tall chain link fence, we find ourselves filing into a line of traffic attempting to enter the base. When we're still about 20 yards away from the main gate, a camouflaged soldier approaches the driver's side window.

He motions for Jim to lower the window. The soldier's bored eyes land on me briefly before focusing on Jim. "I'm Private First-Class Mitchell. What is your purpose here today?"

Jim plasters an innocent smile on his face. "We were hoping you all could help us. It's me and my wife here," he says, motioning toward me. I almost miss his next words as I stifle a gag. "And my brother, he's hurt." He nods toward the back of the RV. "He sure could use some medical attention. Stat." He chuckles with that last word. Since when did Jim start cracking jokes? Maybe he does that when he knows he's not in charge.

"Well, you're in luck," Mitchell says, looking between us.

"This base is still open to civilians seeking refuge. And we do have medical facilities on site."

We park the RV and climb out, leaving Dan inside. We don't dare lift him and brush against the bulging wounds on his skin. Within a few minutes, medics appear. When they see the condition he's in, they agree to take him directly to the infirmary.

They carefully extract Dan and whisk him away on a stretcher. My heart knows this is the best thing for him. Even if it's not for me. He's going to be okay now that we're here.

Mitchell guides us toward a second, smaller gate I hadn't noticed before. It shoots off from the main entrance, although it's not labeled. We approach an area with makeshift barriers set up to form lines, like an amusement park ride.

The now-empty lines lead to a bank of metal detectors. Mitchell motions for us to proceed, so we wind our way through the queue.

"I got keys in my pocket. They gonna make this thing go off?" Jim asks hesitantly.

"No," Mitchell says proudly. Patting the circular column of the closest metal detector, he explains, "These are high tech. They know to ignore nuisance alarm triggers like keys, coins, and belt buckles." With that, he nods once, encouraging us to walk through.

Jim motions to me. "Ladies first," he says, smiling. When did he decide to start using manners?

I start through the gray pillars but freeze when the connecting bar at the top emits a steady beeping and flashing red lights. Ugh. The knife. The stupid knife I shoved in my shoe. It found a semi-comfortable niche in the crook of my arch and I completely forgot about it.

Mitchell cocks his head to the side, evaluating me. Nearby soldiers watch but don't come closer. Jim narrows his eyes and takes a step back, as if subconsciously distancing himself from me.

"Ma'am, please step over to the side," Mitchell commands. "Are you carrying any metal on your person?"

I almost laugh. Almost. Yep, I've got a knife, but it did me no good.

Chapter 26

Jim's jaw drops in shock when I slowly slide the knife out of my shoe. Mitchell steps closer and I gladly hand the weapon over to him. I calmly explain how and why I had the knife, stressing that I didn't actually use it.

Mitchell asks me to place my hands against the wall and he performs a brief pat-down, asking me if I have any other weapons. Once Jim and I successfully pass through the metal detectors, another soldier approaches and escorts us to Intake Office 2.

As we step into the drab trailer, a nameless face directs us to sit across from him at a desk. This whole base is becoming a blur. I half-listen as he asks questions about who we are, where we're from, and our intentions on the base. Jim answers for both of us and the soldier types away on a keyboard, documenting all of Jim's lies.

My eyes rove around the room. Two simple metal desks sit in opposite corners of the space. A mess of folding chairs, just like the ones we sit in, are scattered before each desk. Random camouflaged soldiers enter and exit the office, paying us no attention.

I watch as one of them approaches a tall beige cabinet standing at attention against the wall. He unlocks the door and carefully pulls it toward him. Metallic squeaking pierces the room. The solider across the desk from us loudly clears his throat, pulling our attention back to him.

"Alright, that about wraps things up here," the soldier says, rising from his chair. "Next stop is the medical center. All civilians get a rudimentary physical and a vaccination." That catches my attention.

"A vaccination for what?" I ask, meeting his eyes for the first time. He scratches his head nonchalantly.

"Just a precaution, ma'am, to avoid spreading illness to the vulnerable populations." Under his breath, he adds, "Lots more people living here these days, lots more germs. Last thing we need is an outbreak on base."

I didn't think of it that way. I wonder how many people are here and how many more will come.

Jim shoots me a cautionary gaze. His meaning is crystal clear: don't argue, just do what they ask. The soldier directs us to the medical building and sends us on our way.

As we follow signs throughout the field, Jim talks just loud enough for me to hear but low enough that others would never be able to make out his words. He grasps my hand as if we're a happy couple that just found their salvation.

"Riley, you probably know that Dan and I did some stuff back home. Stuff we had to do to survive." He shoots a skeptical glance my way.

Yeah right. Quinn and I were surviving just fine and we didn't have to murder anyone to steal their food.

"Anyway," he continues, squeezing my hand a little harder. "The point is, Riley, I did what I had to do. Now, these people need to believe that we're together." His eyebrows rise expectantly.

"I get it, okay?" I concede, crossing my arms.

"Do you? Cuz I'm not so sure you do," his voice momentarily rises but he extinguishes his anger just as quickly. "For this to work, we need to be what we say we are," he says. "I want to see an Academy Award winning performance out of you," he threatens, his eyes darkening.

I wonder if that's the last thing Mrs. Adams saw before he stabbed her to death.

Chapter 27

Our first stop is the hospital. A white paper sign taped to the entrance directs us inside. The white block letters instruct us to sit and wait to be called. I follow Jim to the nearest row of hard plastic chairs and lower myself into one.

Drab gray walls frame a rectangle of about a dozen black chairs. Less than half are filled with bodies. I let my hands drop to my lap while my eyes explore the room. A little girl, probably around six or seven years old, stares at me. Her parents are talking to each other in another language, but her dark eyes remain fixed on me.

When I flash a smile, her eyes drop to the floor for several seconds before she returns a shy glance. She clutches a blue stuffed unicorn with a few yellow and pink spots. We both turn when a creaking door opens and a camouflage-clad soldier steps out. Her black hair is slicked back into a tight bun. The stethoscope dangling from her neck is the only indication that she is part of the medical personnel.

The woman strides toward the little girl's parents and extends a hand. "Mr. and Mrs. Tran?" she asks tentatively. When they nod, she continues. "I'm Officer Harris. Follow me, please, and we'll get you taken care of so you can get settled in your quarters."

As I watch the little girl trail behind her parents and into the room with Officer Harris, a warm hand clamps down over mine. "Riley," Jim commands my attention. "Stop wringing your hands like that." I squint in momentary confusion, but awareness returns and, sure enough, my hands have a mind of their own.

I shake my head, as if brushing off his words. He doesn't own me. "It's just a nervous habit, Jim. I don't even realize I'm doing it. It's not a big deal."

Through gritted teeth he whispers, "It makes you look nervous. You shouldn't be nervous, Riley. You know you're safe here with your husband." His eyes dare me to argue. Instead, I adopt a bored stance and slouch into the stiff chair.

About ten minutes later, the small family emerges from their meeting. The little girl cradles her stuffed unicorn, twirling a purple lollipop with her other hand.

"Mei, honey, wait right there," the slender woman calls to the little girl. She and the man linger at the doorway, still talking to whoever is in there. A soft voice pulls my attention to the silky-haired girl standing before me.

"You're pretty," the little girl, Mei, says. Brushing a lock of hair behind my ear, I flash her a genuine smile. Her eyes dart to my scar for just a moment.

"Thank you. You know you're very beautiful yourself," I say.

She smiles shyly, her eyes dropping to the floor. I poke the stuffed unicorn and ask, "And who is this?"

Her shyness dissolves as she excitedly introduces me to Mr. Sparkles.

Jim huffs in boredom but I ignore him.

"Mr. Sparkles wants to ask you a question," she says innocently. I pretend to tickle the unicorn's belly and meet his sparkly purple eyes.

"What is it, Mr. Sparkles?" I ask.

Lifting the stuffed animal in front of her face, Mei attempts a deep voice that sounds more adorably ridiculous than masculine. "What happened to your cheek?"

I'm so startled by the question that I'm momentarily dumbfounded. With a sharp intake of breath, I raise a hand to my cheek, tracing the scar. I almost forgot, for just a moment, that my cheek bears a huge gash. Now it's going to be the first thing people notice when they look at my face.

Mei nervously peeks around Mr. Sparkles, either awaiting my response or gauging my reaction. Maybe both. Before I can form any words, Jim answers for me.

"Don't you worry about it, little girl. You mind your own business," Jim snaps. "I think it's time to find your mommy and daddy." He pauses for a moment before shooing her away. "Go on now."

A little hand raises, as if to wave goodbye, just as her parents spring forward to retrieve her. Her mother's dark complexion exudes concern.

"Mei, honey, are you bothering these people?"

Before the little girl can answer, I sharply shake my head.

"No, not at all," I say, rising from the seat. "Mei was kind enough to introduce me to Mr. Sparkles. He's a very handsome fellow."

The woman breathes a sigh of relief and runs a slender hand through her dark wavy hair. "Oh good. Alright, well, it's time for us to go. Come on, sweetie." As her parents head for the door, Mei trails behind them. She throws me a smile and a genuine wave before the door closes behind her.

Before I have a chance to return to my seat, a uniformed woman pops out of a door and announces that she's ready to see Riley Masters.

Chapter 28

Laptop in hand, the doctor steps into the waiting room and scans it for her next patient. I slowly rise from my chair, surprised she's calling us back individually. Jim shoots to his feet. "I should come too, I'm her...husband." It's so wrong that even he stumbles over the word.

"Sir, we will be with you in a moment. Right now, I am ready to see..." she starts as her eyes dance across the laptop. Scrutinizing my eyes, she concludes, "Riley Masters. Is that correct?"

One heartbeat and deep gulp later, I nod dumbly, focusing on holding her gaze. Does she suspect something?

Her eyes quickly scan my cheek and stained shirt, silently assessing. I'll bet she misses nothing. I'm not fooling her with the old "turn-the-shirt-inside-out" trick.

"Well, Riley Masters, it is very nice to meet you. I am Dr. Noori but please call me Safiya." She throws Jim a dismissive nod and turns on her heel. "Mrs. Masters, right this way."

I follow her to a small exam room. Other than the stethoscope looped around her neck, she looks like any other soldier, covered in camouflage. Smooth mocha skin complements her deep brown eyes. Her black hair is pulled into a tight bun at the nape of her neck.

"That's a really pretty name, Dr. N—um, Safiya," I stammer. When her eyes drop to my lap, I know I'm wringing my hands again. I've got to acknowledge the awkwardness. Shaking my hands out, I force out a slight chuckle.

"I'm sorry, I'm just nervous. It's been…a rough road to get here." At least that's not a lie.

"I understand, and you are safe now." She pauses momentarily, swiping the laptop's screen. Her eyes glance over what I can only imagine is a description of my grand entrance. Though she maintains a professional air, I notice her eyes jump a few times as she reads the available information.

"So," she says in a thick accent. "You made quite the entrance when you arrived here." Her deep brown eyes radiate kindness and amusement. I can't help but smile at her. Her articulate enunciation of each word sounds strange. I'm used to slang and sloppy English. While her words are measured, her demeanor is genuinely warm.

"It sounds like both you, and another person you arrived with, had injuries. And, you were carrying a weapon." She watches me carefully, letting the silence invite me to explain.

"Um…yeah," I stammer. "You know it can be pretty

dangerous out there," I say while shakily pointing toward the door. I slide my hands under my thighs to prevent the inevitable wringing acrobatics they'll attempt next.

"I would imagine so," she says politely. "Let me ask. Did the weapon cause any of the injuries?" I didn't expect that question.

"No! No, I just had the knife to protect myself, that's all. I didn't actually use it on anyone." My nerves electrify, triggering my hands to tremble with worry. I wonder what she thinks of me, showing up here with dried blood crusted on my clothes and a knife in my shoe.

"Do you know where Dan is? Is he okay?" She's got to know something.

"We are going to get him fixed up," Safiya says, placing a hand on my shoulder. "Tell me, Riley, are you related to Daniel? I cannot release patient information except to relatives."

"Yes," I start, I can't believe I'm about to say this, "Um, yeah, Dan's my brother-in-law so I'm family. And he was in pretty bad shape when we arrived. He was swarmed by fire ants, we think."

She gently places a cold palm over my hand. "I assure you we are going to do everything we can to help him." Her eyes speak honesty. If she told me the sky was green right now, I'd probably believe her. Although maybe that isn't so far-fetched at the moment.

Looking down at her laptop, she swipes a few screens. "Daniel Masters is in the isolation ward," she says. "We have to conduct some testing on him before we can move him to a regular bed." I open my mouth to ask when he'll be out of isolation and what kind of tests they're running on him, but she continues before I can utter a word.

"But we are here to talk about you right now." She stares at me intently, reaching for my scarred cheek. "May I?"

I nod quickly.

She gently tugs on green medical gloves. After a quick examination, she steps to an adjacent counter and proceeds to open several drawers, retrieving supplies: a bottle of antiseptic, swabs, and tube of what looks like glue. Walking back toward me, she holds my gaze.

"Now, why don't you tell me about how this happened?" she asks, her eyes as inquisitive as her words. She sets to work as I talk, explaining how Dylan and his friends broke into the RV. I leave out the part about how it wasn't exactly our RV to begin with, and about what happened with Alex.

My voice quakes with each word and tears blur my vision. She asks a few questions, like how long ago this happened, but she doesn't pry. When I finish talking, she gives me a wistful look.

"And your parents are…not here with you?" she asks carefully. I shake my head. Forcing an upbeat turn to the conversation, she smiles.

"You know, Mrs. Riley, you do not need a weapon to be strong." She pauses momentarily, letting that sink in. "You can work to make this," she points to her brain, "and this," she taps on her bicep, "strong. And those are the very best weapons any of us have."

"Now, enough distracting me," she teases. "Let's clean and close that wound."

With a genuine smile, stretching some facial muscles that haven't gotten much use in several weeks, I nod.

Chapter 29

The last two days have been a blur. I've alternated between visiting the library to checking on Dan in the hospital. After the first day, he was moved out of isolation. They figured out pretty quickly that he wasn't contagious. And with some anti-inflammatory medication, the swelling went way down. He's still weak and on a steady stream of painkillers, but he's conscious and healing. For that, I am thankful.

This base is like a mini town. Everything we need is tucked safely within the perimeter fence—a recreation center, dry cleaner, gas station, fast food restaurants and a grocery store, or commissary, as they call it. There's even a bowling alley and small movie theater.

I have no interest in leisure activities, except for reading. It's my only escape.

Jim and I share a room, since we're supposedly married. Thankfully, since there are only so many rooms available, we had to take one that mimics a standard cadet dorm room—with two separate beds and two desks. Once we were processed, my next fear was that I'd have to share a bed with Jim.

Mostly, my time is spent in the mess hall or our assigned room. And Jim is by my side through it all. Yesterday he decided to check out the base's gym, so I tagged along. The whole place felt foreign. I always hated gym class and I was never athletic. But something about Safiya's words stay with me. The only way out of this is to get stronger.

No one is coming to rescue me. This isn't living. It's just going through the motions—sleeping, eating, breathing. And I'm not sure how much longer I can do it.

With a few hours to kill before dinner, I decide to visit Dan. Of course, Jim has to accompany me. Although we pass people along the way, they might as well have purple skin and green hair. I don't see faces or personalities. I just follow the path to the hospital, barely acknowledging the surroundings.

With each step, I retreat further into my mind. I should start working out at that gym. Safiya's right. I can work on making myself stronger. It's not like we're going to live on this base forever. This is a temporary stop. Once everything gets fixed outside, we'll leave. It's a long way home, and I need to be ready to go whenever a chance to escape comes.

A harsh antiseptic smell bombards my senses the moment the sliding glass doors swish open. Walking through the spotless hallways, we proceed to room 304, Dan's temporary home.

Pushing through the wooden door, I smile when I see the patient.

For the first time since we've been on the base, Dan greets us from his bed. Propped at a forty-degree angle, his eyes dance when they recognize our faces. Jim rushes past me and clasps his brother on the shoulder.

"You're looking good, brother!"

Dan's smile prompts a genuine grin to burst across my face. He's really going to be okay. His skin still screams with abrasions from the fire ants, but he's improved tremendously. We never could have saved him without this place.

Taking seats next to the bed, we listen as Dan updates us on his day, and how they were able to cut back some of his pain medication. When he finishes, his jovial mood turns somber.

I stand, intending to place a hand over his but hesitate when I remember his scorched skin.

His eyes shift between us. "When I was, like, really out of it," he starts hesitantly. "I think I heard some stuff. Stuff about the base."

My narrowed eyes flick to Jim instinctively and his meet mine.

"What kind of stuff did you hear?" I ask gently. I get the feeling he thinks we won't believe him.

Releasing a deep breath, he continues. "It's almost full. They're gonna close it soon. We're sure as hell lucky we got here when we did." He smirks but it's weak.

My worry reflects in his eyes. What will happen if others, like us, are out there looking for a place to go?

Our conversation is cut short when a nurse arrives to deliver medication. Noting that it's getting close to dinner time, she encourages us to come back tomorrow so that her patient can rest. We say our goodbyes and walk in silence back to our room.

My mind whirls with this new information. If Dan's better, maybe he'll help me get away from Jim. He knows I don't want to be here. Maybe he'll even come with me.

I silence that thought before I allow my brain to slither too far down that path. Dan may be a good guy who's just had a lousy influence his whole life, but he'd still never leave his brother. I know that because if I can make it back to Quinn, I'm not leaving her side again. Ever.

Chapter 30

A sharp wrapping on our door pulls me out of my latest library find. Jim's eyes meet mine before he scrambles up and yanks it open. He takes two automatic steps back when a solider greets him.

"Sir, I am here to see Riley Masters."

Again, Jim glances my way. Neither of us responds in stunned silence. Since we arrived here, we have had no visitors. We're free to roam the base as long as we stay out of authorized areas, but no one checks on us. The necessities are provided to us, so we haven't had to worry about money.

"And what is this about?" Jim asks cautiously.

"Someone wants to speak to her. Privately," the soldier says, making it pretty clear that Jim isn't invited.

Scrunching my face in confusion, I fashion an honest response. "Why would anyone here want to talk to me?" As soon as the words pass my lips, I feel Jim's red-hot glare turn my way, confirming he's wondering the same thing.

"Look, I have orders to retrieve you," the soldier says impatiently, pointing at me. Turning that pointer finger toward Jim, he finishes with, "And you, sir, are to stay put."

"I'm her husband," Jim pushes. "Doesn't that count for anything around here?"

Stopping just short of rolling his eyes, the soldier huffs out a frustrated breath. Grabbing the radio on his belt, he lifts it to his mouth. Meeting Jim's eyes, he depresses the button.

"Sir, the lady you asked me to retrieve, her husband is demanding that he accompany her," he says.

A stern voice immediately cuts through the mild static. "No. Just her. If he can't follow our orders, then I will personally explain what is expected of guests on this base."

Satisfied, the soldier gives Jim a knowing smirk. "That is my sergeant. If he says, 'Just her,' then that means it's 'just her.'"

Jim's face reddens, but he stays silent. His steely glare threatens what he can't voice in front of the solider. *You better keep your mouth shut.*

Shrugging my shoulders, I concede. "Okay, I'm ready." At least I'll get a few minutes away from my prison cell, also known as *our room.*

Jim's fury chokes the air as the soldier turns on his heel and opens the door for me. I throw Jim another shrug before stepping into the corridor. Pausing to let the soldier lead the way, I follow obediently, letting my eyes wander up and down the drab hallways.

"Now, ma'am, I'm going to bring you to my sergeant, and

he'll take you to see your visitor."

I answer with a slight um-hm. *No one is here to see Riley Whelan. And whoever wants to see Riley Masters is in for a disappointment.*

Lost in my own thoughts, I struggle to keep up with my escort. His legs are much longer than mine and he strides at a fast pace.

As we exit the living quarters and follow the pavement to another building, a calming warmth spreads over my skin. Hope slowly unfolds with each step I take. Maybe it's Safiya who wants to see me? Maybe she suspected something was seriously wrong and wants to help me? Could she help me track down Quinn?

We approach another gray building, its sign labeling it the Family Readiness Center. I no longer struggle to keep up with the soldier. I'm on his heels, ready to see my visitor. When he leads me to a small office, I'm nearly jumping out of my skin in anticipation.

My eagerness plummets when the room's only occupant stands to greet me. It's just another solider. I glance at his name badge: E. Bowen.

"Sir," my escort says. "This is Riley Masters." I look to the new guy and he gives the soldier I came with a sharp nod of dismissal. The soldier marches out of the room, closing the door behind him.

Extending a hand to me, the new guy introduces himself. "I'm Sergeant Bowen. I'd like to have just a word with you before I bring you to your visitor." Motioning to a stiff chair, he says, "Please have a seat."

I comply, numbly dropping into the seat that's just as uncomfortable as it looks.

"So, your name is Riley Masters?" he asks, eyebrows raised.

"Didn't we already establish that?" I reply cautiously. He scratches his chin, scrutinizing my features. *What's he looking for? Does he know my existence here is a lie?*

"Do you have any family members that might be looking for you?" he tries. I hold his gaze. "What are you saying? Is someone really here to see me?" I rise from my seat. I need to know what's going on. Now.

The sergeant blows out a frustrated sigh and stands. "We're not really getting anywhere here anyway," he says under his breath. Walking around the desk, he opens the door for me and we stride back down the dreary hallway.

Questions swirl through my mind as I follow the sergeant. When he stops outside another nondescript door, he glances at me before slowing pushing the door open. Hopefully, there's not another random soldier in this room, just waiting to ask me ridiculous questions.

When he crosses the threshold, I obediently follow. As soon as the sergeant steps aside, my eyes focus on the space before me previously occupied by his solid frame. In that moment they land on the one person I never thought I'd see again.

My heart bubbles with emotion while my mind numbs with shock. *Quinn. It's really Quinn. She found me.* My vision blurs as tears threaten to spill. Silence surrounds us. For all I know we could have a whole audience watching us right now. But I don't care. All I see is my sister, even though she's becoming a splotchy blur with every second that passes.

As I rush toward her, my pulse quickens and thoughts flash through my mind. I am not Riley Masters. I never was. I'm Riley

Whelan. Quinn's older sister. And now that she's here, nothing else matters.

As I collapse into her arms, everything else fades away. A single word bubbles to the surface in my mind. *Home.*

AUTHOR NOTE

Dear Reader,

Thanks for taking the time to catch up with Riley. Although she didn't get much attention in book 1 of the series, *Darkness Falls*, she was just as busy as Quinn and the rest of the gang. And, while Quinn and Riley are back together and all is well for the moment, they sit on the cusp of danger and disorder. If you'd like to join them on their continued journey, stay tuned for book 3 of the Nature's Fury series, *Devastation Erupts*, which will be released in 2020.

If you enjoyed *Anguish Unfolds,* please take a moment to post a review or rating on Amazon and/or Goodreads. Reviews are a HUGE help to independent authors, and they help readers discover books they may have otherwise never found. Even a star rating with no review is appreciated.

Want updates on story progress and other news? Visit my website to sign up for my e-newsletter. Or connect with me on social media – I'm active on Twitter, Instagram, and Facebook.

In the meantime, happy reading!

ACKNOWLEDGEMENTS

Michelle Preast of Indie Book Cover Designs, thank you so much for creating another great cover for my series! I am certain Riley would be pleased with it. ☺

Thank you to my beta readers – I find your input invaluable, and I'm always surprised by how much impact a minor suggestion has on the final story. **Beth Suit of BB Books**, thank you for your thoughtful review of my draft. You definitely keep me on task for adding emotion, and the world will never know how many italics you saved it from! ☺ **Emily Angeline & Robin Asick,** your input definitely makes my scenes stronger and your call for more details—both environmental and emotional—has been heeded. Thank you for accompanying my characters on their journey and being my trusted first readers!

Vanessa Anderson at Night Owl Freelance, what a difference having one book under my belt made! Thank you for your continued support and guidance. Working with you, this process gets easier each time. I look forward to crafting many more stories that will only be improved upon with your input.

Friends & family members, I can't express how much I appreciate your ongoing support. **Robin & Carol**, thank you for continually pushing my books on your unsuspecting friends and colleagues!

Scott, Landon & Aidan, thank you for continuing to support my writing endeavors! I love bouncing ideas off of you and I appreciate your input. ♥

ABOUT THE AUTHOR

A. E. Faulkner was born and raised in Pennsylvania. When she's not lost in a book, she loves spending time with her husband and two sons, especially while hiking, biking, or exploring nature. She loves *almost* everything about nature—ticks excluded, and one of her biggest fears is the repercussions we will face when nature can no longer tolerate human destruction. As such, she never tires of reading dystopian-themed tales. Stories about the end of the world absolutely fascinate her.

FOLLOW HER WORK

To learn more visit:
AuthorAEFaulkner.com

She can also be found:

Tweeting @AuthAEFaulkner

on Facebook @authaefaulkner

& on Instagram @authoraefaulkner

To leave a Goodreads review, please visit
Goodreads.com and search for
Anguish Unfolds by A. E. Faulkner.

DEVASTATION
ERUPTS
BOOK 3 OF THE NATURE'S FURY SERIES
"There's no running from fate when
it's determined to destroy all in its path"
A.E. FAULKNER

DARKNESS
FALLS
BOOK 1 OF THE NATURE'S FURY SERIES
When Mother Nature reaches her breaking point,
humans have no choice but to face her fury.
A.E. FAULKNER